I0631038

The Magician's Walk

LORI ZUPPINGER

Tea & Music

This is a work of fiction. Names, characters, businesses, places, events and incidents are either the product of the author's imagination or used in a fictitious manner. Any resemblance to actual persons, living or dead, or actual events is purely coincidental.

Copyright © 2017 Lori Zuppinger

Tea & Music, Toronto

All rights reserved.

ISBN: 978-0-9959799-2-5

Cover art by Ann McDougall Design & Creative Services

O day and night, but this is wondrous strange!
- William Shakespeare

ACKNOWLEDGMENTS

These don't get any easier to write with the second book, apparently; there are just so many people who have played a role in getting to the point of releasing these stories into the wild.

To Anthony – thank you for your continuing patience, both with the amount of my time that writing takes up, and the fact that I am continuing on with my beloved magicians and not *quite* getting to your favourite steampunk adventure. (Yet. I promise it's on the list.)

To Duncan – sorry about the first book having a few swears in it. This one has a couple too.

To Shelly – thank you for taking the first book on a journey to a whole different set of west coast islands and ferry rides.

Most of all, for all the people who have been kind enough to read The Magicians' Card, share your thoughts, and follow up and ask when the next one is coming out – thank you for giving me the ongoing motivation to jump right back into it. Since the first book was initially drafted, I've spent a few years living part-time in this imaginary world with Heather and the magicians, and I'm delighted that so many people have come to join me here.

CHAPTER ONE

"Are you ready to go?"

Was I? It was a good question. I was still standing with one hand on the doorknob, one hand on the key in the lock. Giving myself a bit of a shake, I took the key out and tucked it in my pocket. One more look at the front of the house and I turned to answer. "Yeah, Dad, I think I am."

Just under two months before, I had set off on a quest of sorts, following an old story and some guesswork, and found the troupe of travelling magicians that I'd known as a tale from my great-grandmother's girlhood. More than that, I had learned that we were linked in ways I could not have imagined, and I had been invited to join their ranks. I was leaving to take them up on it.

None of this, of course, had been completely explained to anyone, in the whirlwind of visits and phone calls and organization that had gone on in my whistle-stop back in Canada. Though the magicians performed to the public, they maintained a veil of secrecy; only a few trusted individuals outside the group knew even a fraction of the story. I had come up with a version to give my family: a sabbatical to do more travelling, and to follow up on a possible work opportunity. That much was more or less true, and fair enough – I was long since grown up, after all, I had ample money saved, and I had no one to truly answer to since the implosion of my marriage the year before. My dad still saw fit to ask more questions, though, even as he drove me to the airport.

"So… you still don't have a firm plan of when you'll be back?"

I didn't, and said so. "We'll see how things go, Dad. Maybe Christmas, but I don't want to make any promises. You know how Mum and Lisa are."

"They mean well; you know that." My mother and sister had been underwhelmed by my plans, particularly once they had gotten the inkling that I might be considering a permanent move. "They worry."

"Lisa thinks it's about Alan. It's not. Not really." I looked out the window as Toronto gradually receded into the background. "I mean, I wouldn't have – I probably wouldn't have discovered some of these possibilities if we were still married, but I'm not breaking up with my life just because my husband turned out to be an asshole. Sorry," I added, at the profanity that had slipped out unthinking. "I think it's really the other way around, that I've always wanted to see more of the world but never had the chance while we were together."

My dad nodded. "It's either in your nature or it isn't, honey. Granny Chrissie always said you were cut out for adventure."

My eyes misted over just a little. Granny Chrissie – my dad's grandmother, my great-grandmother – had been the one to set the whole thing in motion, with her tale of mysterious performers descending on the quiet Isle of Lewis in 1920. Years later, on her deathbed, I had learned that she'd confided the whole story to no other living soul. At the time I'd wondered why I had been chosen out of all her numerous descendants; I still wondered, but along different lines. Had some accident of recessive genetics given the gift of magic to me alone, out of all my aunts and uncles and cousins? Pondering this, I realized I had missed something else my dad had said to me.

"I just wondered how you'll arrange it, if you do decide to stay on," he said, after I asked him to repeat himself. "Is this the sort of thing where they'd be able to get you a work permit?"

My few weeks at home had included a good deal of research; this was a question that had occurred to me as well. "Well, if I want to base myself in the UK, I can apply for an ancestry visa. You have to have at least one British-born grandparent. So I'd need your dad's birth certificate."

"Is that so?" He spared me a quick glance before turning his attention back to the road. "I had no idea that was a possibility. So maybe Don Ross will have been good for something, after all."

Although he said it lightly, I knew he did not have a high opinion of his father. Don Ross had been a 'hard man'; by all accounts my gran had been better off without him. As it happened, I had come to know some things about my paternal grandfather that my dad would not. I wondered how he would react if I revealed that Don's unmarried mother had been my Granny Chrissie's childhood friend. That both girls had been romanced by the same magician, though only one had been left with an unexpected souvenir. And especially the fact that this same magician had only just passed away a few short weeks before, giving me his final blessing before drawing his last breath at the truly improbable age of one hundred and thirty-eight. I thought of all this and knew that there was no good way to reveal it, and nothing to be served from sharing that knowledge.

Instead, I changed the subject. "Dad, you've been to Dublin before. Did you ever go up to the Hill of Tara?"

CHAPTER TWO

The Hill of Tara. *Three weeks. Don't be late*, Eric had said, as he'd handed me his magician's card with the location and a phone number on the reverse. Eric Heyward had been my first point of contact with the magicians – though it was only on our third meeting that he had dropped a clue to his real identity. He had taken me under his wing, suspecting the existence of my gift well before I had any idea of it, and had been one of the loudest voices encouraging me to join them. It made sense that he'd been the one to give me this essential bit of information, hastily written on a calling card: where to find them next.

Sitting in the departure lounge at Pearson, I pulled the card out and looked at it for probably the thousandth time. *A troupe of MAGICIANS from parts unknown – Nightly Performances to Astound and Amaze!* The text had been the same on the card passed to my Granny Chrissie in 1920, though hers had been torn and faded by the time I'd found it in her jewelry box at the age of thirteen. I wondered when the line had first been used, and how long the group had been plying their trade.

This card was thoroughly modern, though, with an overseas phone number that had to be Eric's cell. During my weeks at home, it had occurred to me that I could phone him at any time, but I had shied away from the idea, in much the same way that I'd resisted the impulse to search his name on social media. I wasn't ready yet to blur the boundaries between magic and what I couldn't help thinking of as 'real life'. And I wanted my return to be in the old-fashioned, simple way: just showing up. The phone number was something I would save as a contingency plan.

By the time I stepped out of Dublin Airport at the other end, it was nearly noon. I managed to find a bus into the city easily enough, and asked at the terminal how to get to Tara. "The one-oh-nine to Navan and alight at Tara Cross, dear," the grey-haired ticket clerk told me. "It runs every half-hour; every fifteen minutes at the afternoon peak."

I had originally planned to go there direct from the airport, but on the plane I had thought of Eric's other instruction: *get a phone next time*. As much as I cherished the idea of turning up unannounced, I had to admit it made sense to have modern technology as a fallback position. It was a reasonably quick errand to set my phone up with a new SIM card and a local phone number that was liable to take me forever to memorize. If I had been in Dublin with any other motive, I would have spent time sightseeing, but by four-thirty I was boarding the 109 bus. *Don't be late*. I was already a few days past the three weeks I'd guessed for my return, and it would be dusk by seven-thirty or so. I wanted to make my re-entry before the show got completely underway for the evening.

As I watched the fringes of the city slip by the bus window, I wondered what my odds would be of finding Eric first, or another of my small handful of friends among the troupe. Eric's half-sister Claire, or Ben, his biological father. Or maybe Luke, the charming nineteen-year-old troublemaker who'd turned out to be some kind of distant cousin of mine. I knew all too well that there were at least a few others who would not be so welcoming of my return, though. When the impossibly elderly Raffaele had revealed on his deathbed not only that he was my great-grandfather, but that my Granny Chrissie had been the illegitimate child of Sébastien, apparently one of the greatest magicians in living memory, he had left quite a bombshell in his wake. Raffaele's daughter Isabella had been livid that I had been the one to receive his dying blessing, that – purely by accident as far as I was concerned – I'd been the one at his side when he breathed his last. Perhaps her anger had cooled over the intervening weeks, but I didn't want to hasten the moment of finding out.

Outside the city limits, the vista opened into farms, gently undulating off to the horizon. If it were not for the narrowness of the road and how closely it was hemmed in by greenery, the view might have resembled the southern Ontario landscape of my childhood. About forty-five minutes into the trip, I glimpsed a sign saying that Tara was eight kilometres away. My pulse began to speed up, and I scanned the surroundings with greater interest. The closer we got, the more I expected to see a glimpse of tents, a van with a banner, any hint that the magicians had not been a figment of my imagination. A few minutes later, the bus slowed to a halt just past a sign for Tara pointing up a small side road. "Tara Cross," the driver announced, as I hastily pulled my backpack down from the overhead rack. Thanking her, I stepped down and stood knee-deep in the tall grass at the roadside as the bus lumbered away.

There was no one in sight. Once the bus disappeared round a bend, there was not a vehicle on the road, nor any sign of life in the one house nearest the bus stop. Granted, this was not so different from some of the rural places I'd encountered in Scotland, and it was only five-thirty; there was no reason to expect traffic to be heading to see the magicians yet. Shouldering my bag, I headed in the direction the signpost indicated.

It was a narrow lane, closely bordered much of the way by hedges and trees; beyond these, I saw another five or six well-kept farmhouses as I made my way up the increasing incline. My first sight of another human being was when I had to edge almost into the bushes to get out of the way of a tractor coming in the opposite direction; the driver gave a cheery wave as he passed. After ten minutes or so, the lane opened out onto another road that was flanked on both sides by parking; a coach sat across several spaces, its door open as the last of a line of people filed back inside. A pair of buildings off to my left looked to be a gift shop and café, and to the right I could see a closed gate with a narrow pedestrian access beside it, and a path leading on.

The ground sloped downwards in the direction from which I had come, and ahead of me it continued gently up. Nowhere in my view was there any evidence of a travelling circus. If my experience at Callanish was anything to judge by, they would want to be within sight of the monuments; perhaps they were set up somewhere on the other side of the hill.

A sign indicated that the visitor centre was closed after mid-September, but the access beside the gate was open. I slipped through and followed up the path, which led me first past a church before taking me to the top of the hill. There, I found a small hillock that looked to have been a tomb, and ancient earthworks forming a rough figure-eight, with a standing stone within one of the rings. Glancing over my shoulder, I reached out to touch the stone, laying my palm flat upon it. I thought I could feel a low thrum, although nothing like what I had experienced at the Callanish stones.

But even from this higher ground, there was no sign of the expected tents, not in any direction I cared to look. I told myself that maybe they were just a little further off, but in my heart of hearts I felt a sense of dread. Was I too late? Had I been wrong to come? The weight of the cell phone in my side pocket was suddenly a reassurance. Finding Eric's card again, I entered the number he had written down, and sent a simple text: *It's Heather. I'm at Tara, where are you?*

Waiting for an answer felt like an eternity, but it was probably only two minutes before the phone pinged with a response: *Long story. Will be there in about an hour. There's a café by the gate, meet you there.*

For the moment, that would have to be enough. It wasn't the surprise return I had envisioned, but at least I wasn't completely stranded in an unfamiliar country. With time to kill, I considered wandering around the hill a little longer, but once the initial surge of panic abated, my stomach reminded me that I had not eaten anything since the pastry I'd grabbed on the way out of the airport several hours before. The café was probably a good idea.

Thankfully, it was open. One elderly couple in almost-matching sweaters sat at a table by the bar, and a waitress appeared when I walked in, but the room was otherwise empty. Over soup, a sandwich and a cup of strong black tea, I contemplated what would happen next. I figured an hour's walk could mean five or six kilometres away, or were they somewhere beyond walking distance? Or perhaps I had simply caught Eric in the midst of doing something and he needed some time before he could come and collect me.

Long before the hour elapsed, I was looking up expectantly each time the bell chimed to signal the door opening – but each time, it announced the entry of couples and families coming for dinner. Finally, just before seven, a slightly battered grey hatchback pulled up and backed into a parking spot just at the edge of what I could see out the window; I couldn't tell who was driving or see them as they exited the car, but a few seconds later the bell rang.

It was a familiar face, but not the one I had expected.

Claire stood in the doorway, looking younger than I remembered in her faded jeans and flax-coloured cardigan, freckled face bare of makeup, hair in a braid wound up loosely on the back of her head. Her eyes swept the room before finding me at the small table in the corner.

"Heather, I got here as quickly as I could. Sorry to keep you waiting around."

"Where's Eric?" I asked, gesturing for her to sit.

She took a deep breath, and was forestalled from replying by the arrival of the waitress. After glancing at my not-quite-finished supper, she ordered a cup of coffee, then watched the woman walk away before turning back to me. "Eric got called home, to America," she said at last. "A week ago – the same day we all arrived here. We'd no sooner got the tents up than he came to me and my dad, said there was a family emergency and he had to go, on the first flight he could get. He left his mobile with me, in case you needed to get in touch."

"Have you heard from him? Is everything okay?"

She frowned. "It's his dad, that's all I know. He didn't know when he'd be back. It seemed bad, though, from the way he looked when he left. I think... well, I don't know. But I think he'll just come back when he's ready; I don't expect he'll be thinking to call us until things are settled – one way or the other. He knows the next few places we're to go."

I looked down at my cup of tea. Eric was in his fifties, as much as he didn't look it; his father – the adoptive father who had raised him, that is – must be in his mid-seventies at least. From the sounds of things, it was entirely possible that he had gotten the worst possible summons: that his dad might be dying, or dead. Claire was right: if that was the case, we had no right to expect him to check in. "Wow. I hope he's alright," I faltered. "I'm glad he thought to leave his phone, or I don't know how I would have found you. Is it far away?"

Claire paused for a moment to pour more cream into her coffee. "Well, there's more," she said, her spoon clinking against the thick earthenware. "Like I said, long story. We're not here anymore. The show came down after two nights."

"Eric said not to be late," I replied, as much to myself as to her. "He wasn't kidding, I guess."

She shook her head. "It wasn't expected. It's…" Looking around at the increasingly crowded restaurant, she pursed her lips. "Maybe it's best if I explain on the way."

I paid the bill as she finished her coffee, and followed her out to the car, nearly getting into the driver's seat before I remembered what side of the road they drove on. "Is something wrong?" I asked, as soon as we were on our way.

She didn't answer immediately, watching carefully down the road as she navigated the narrow lane I had walked up earlier. After we'd turned onto the main road, she glanced at me for a second. "Nothing so bad. It's just… awkward to explain in front of people. Regular people. Well… you know at Callanish, how the stones have their energy?"

Remembering our last night there, the visible aura of power radiating out from the central standing stone and encompassing everyone around, I nodded. "It'd be hard to forget. Your dad told me that it's where you – we – get some of the power from. Like recharging a battery. That's partly what you were coming here for, right?"

"Right. And we haven't been here in years, not since before I went off to uni - long before I first started performing."

"Are all the places so long between visits?" I asked. I already knew they only turned up at Callanish every eighteen or nineteen years.

Claire shook her head. "It depends. Some places, some times, are special. Most places we go more often than Callanish, if that's what you're thinking. Some places just once and don't bother going back. Tara… has had its problems. There were protests for years, when they were planning to put a motorway right up close to it, so we stayed away."

"Not the kind of publicity you want to get involved in."

"Exactly," she replied. "Well, they did go ahead and put the motorway through. This one, in fact." We were approaching a highway interchange; she pulled onto it, in the direction signposted for Dublin. "It's been in for a couple of years now and things have settled down, so I guess they decided to come back. Test the waters."

"And...?"

She sighed. "I don't know, exactly. My dad has some ideas about it – says that all the road works maybe cut through something – but the long and short of it is that the power is gone. Well, not gone completely, but it's like a tap that's lost its pressure. It's weak."

I took a moment to process this. "Will it come back, do you think?"

"My dad thinks so, with enough time, but I take it some people disagreed. Anyhow, between that, and Isabella's lot still mourning Raffaele, and Eric leaving... they made the decision to close up shop. Take a break."

"Who decides that sort of thing?"

Claire sped up to pass a truck, then replied. "There's a few. Elders, most people call them. Sofia's one, obviously – you remember her, the oracle? - and my gran and granddad, though they're not always travelling with us anymore. Isabella. A few others. They kind of set our course. I mean, it's not a dictatorship," she added. "People can give opinions, and no one's obliged to go along to every stop. But this time, I think it was pretty obvious to everyone that the time wasn't right."

When it became clear that she had finished with her account, I asked the next obvious question. "And where are we going now?"

"I should have told you!" she said, laughing. "Sorry, there was so much to catch you up on, I forgot that I was kind of bundling you into the car without even seeing if you wanted to come along. We figured you might not have a place to stay for now, so we've a spare bed for you at Fernwood. My grandparents' farm," she explained. "Mum and Dad are there as well."

"And you?" I asked. "I thought you lived in Dublin when you weren't performing?"

"I have friends I stay with, sometimes," she said. "The way I'm always travelling, it doesn't make sense to keep a flat of my own. But I don't like to descend on them unexpected, and Fernwood's got plenty of space. It's my real home, I guess."

"Where is it?"

"Not so far out of the city, actually. It's in County Wicklow, near a little place called Annamoe. You're welcome to stay as long as you like." We drove on in silence for a while before she spoke again. "I'm sure this isn't the homecoming you were expecting, Heather – but I'm glad you've come back."

CHAPTER THREE

The highway took us round the outskirts of Dublin and further south, before Claire's route led off onto a series of increasingly small country roads. Eventually, she turned down a laneway no wider than the one near Tara. It was nearly full dark by this time – very dark indeed without streetlights – and I thanked my lucky stars that no one was expecting me to get behind the wheel. I saw lights of houses only occasionally.

"We're here," she said, pulling off. "Do you mind opening the gate?"

I climbed out and took a moment to figure out how to unlatch the heavy wooden gate. Stepping back and letting the car pass, I could see gnarled old trees illuminated by the headlamps; well beyond them, I could make out lighted windows. A couple more minutes down the bumpy gravel drive, and we pulled up in front of the house. It was far larger than I'd expected, and not at all what I would have pictured as a 'farmhouse': a two-story stone building, with dormers in the attic above, squarely-built and substantial. "Wow," was all I could say for the moment.

"See? Lots of room," Claire replied, opening the hatch so that I could extract my backpack. "The house is from seventeen-something, but it was half fallen apart when Gran and Granddad bought it in the 'thirties."

For a second, I was tempted to ask her how old her grandparents were, but I was diverted by the opening of the big front door. A moment later, I was being greeted and ushered inside by the grandfather in question. Tall for an older man, he had a wiry build and wore his white hair slicked back with pomade.

"Thank you so much for letting me stay here, Mr…" I trailed off. "I'm sorry; this is embarrassing, but I don't know your last name."

He laughed, and I suddenly saw the resemblance to Ben – and Eric – more clearly. "Do you not? Well, then. It's Kavanagh. Daniel Kavanagh."

"Heather Ross," I replied, hiking up my shoulder so that my backpack didn't fall off as I shook his hand.

"Oh, I know." He tapped his temple with one finger. "We've heard a great deal about you, we have."

"Daniel!" came a voice from behind him. A small, matronly lady was standing in a doorway at the far end of the entrance hall. "Don't keep her talking in the hallway, now. Come through, love, and have a cup of tea; you've had a long enough day, I'm sure. The auld man would keep you there all night if you let him get away with it."

"Thank you, Mrs. Kavanagh." I followed her into what turned out to be the kitchen, the centerpiece of which was a truly enormous old-fashioned stove, the likes of which I'd only seen on old BBC shows, fitted into what once had been an equally massive hearth.

"Molly. Call me Molly, love. Mrs. Kavanagh was my mother-in-law, God rest her soul. Sit down, sit down," she added, gesturing to the scuffed wooden table. "Have you had any supper?"

Although I answered in the affirmative, she brought over a plate of bread, butter and cheese before putting the kettle on. Claire made a gesture suggesting that there was no point in arguing, and pulled up the chair beside mine. "Is there any more stew, Gran? Heather's eaten, but I only had time for a cup of coffee."

With a scandalized sort of noise, Molly took the lid from a large pot on the back of the range and dished up a bowl. "I'd get up and get it," Claire murmured under her breath, "but Gran's a force unto herself. It's best to just let her get on with it."

"My great-gran was much the same," I replied, stifling a chuckle.

"I swear, you young things think you can get by on coffee and naught else, half the time," Molly said with a sigh, before calling out the kitchen door for Daniel. "Go on and tell Ben and Colleen that Heather's here, then."

Relative silence descended for a few minutes as Molly pottered about making the tea and Claire ate her stew; I took the chance to take a better look around the room. The former hearth, the beamed ceiling and stone floor spoke to the age of the house, but much of the rest of the fittings must have been put in when Molly and Daniel bought the place. The sage-painted wooden cabinets, ivy-pattern wallpaper and checkerboard backsplash would have been the latest fashion in the 1930s. Only the oversized refrigerator gave a nod to the twenty-first century. It was, quite possibly, the homiest room I had ever been in. Though I was still rattled by the unexpected turn of events, there were certainly worse places to be.

"There, now." Molly set down a tray with a large brown teapot and three proper cups and saucers, like the ones my Granny Chrissie would have used. "I'm sure I'll have to brew another pot when the others turn up, but meanwhile, Heather: how are you holding up, my dear?" She sat down at last, across the table from me, and patted my hand. "It must have been a bit of a shock."

"A bit. But I guess I knew things were going to be a bit unpredictable, when I decided to get myself into this."

She shook her head, making her short white curls bounce. "Just such terrible timing. Thank heavens Eric thought to leave his phone, or who knows when you would have found us. It's always such a risk letting someone new go off, not knowing if they're even certain to be back. When Eric first came to us, Ben was worried sick every time they parted ways, until we knew for sure that he was going to stay. I don't think you were given the luxury of such a long time to come to a decision, though, were you? Isabella wouldn't have let them."

I nodded. "I have the feeling she would have preferred that I never showed my face again, under the circumstances."

Molly waved her hand. "Ah. Don't pay it too much mind. Isabella blows hot and cold, and she was devoted to her old dad, more so than the rest of them. She'll need some time to figure out what she's to do now. I still can't believe he's gone, myself."

"Did you know him well?" I was still trying to guess at the math in my head. Eric was fifty-three. Ben – his biological father – though he looked like a young sixty, therefore had to be into his seventies at the very least, and quite probably older. So that meant that Molly and Daniel, who might be eighty to a casual observer, must be somewhere more in the neighbourhood of a hundred, at a conservative estimate. It was not outside the realm of possibility that they might be contemporaries of my notorious great-grandfather Raffaele, born in 1875 and buried in 2013.

"Well enough. I'd decided that I'd marry Daniel from the time I was six years old and he was eight – though it took him till my twenty-first birthday to work up the nerve to ask me – so Raffaele never paid me much mind when we were young. He saved his flattery for outsider girls, anyhow; that much easier to impress them with magic when they can't do it themselves. But over the years... you can't live half the year in caravans with a hundred or so people, without getting to know them all well enough." She looked off into the middle distance, shaking her head gently. "It's not nearly so rough now, but it's still like a little village when it comes down to it. You'll get to know them all in your time, too. But here, I'm going off the road; you were asking after Raffaele. I never approved of the way he chased after the girls, especially the ones too young and poor to know much better. He thought so long as he went to Confession now and then, his account was clean, but not so much for the girl who might find a baby coming and him long gone."

I thought of Ina Ross, left as a single mum in 1920s Glasgow. "Indeed."

From the sympathetic look she gave me, I was sure that Molly knew the thorny tale of my family tree. "But apart from that," she resumed, "if you didn't know about his romances, you'd think he was a fine man. Always had a friendly word for you. He was devoted to Sébastien. Some might have thought a little too much, considering." She coughed politely. "The thing is, Raffaele was so young when Sébastien found him, and his life had been hard... and so he worshipped the man. I honestly think that Sébastien was the one who taught him to be a philanderer, just as much as he taught him to be a great magician. And he did love his family, above all, especially once Sébastien died. Raffaele had his faults, for certain, but in his heart he wasn't an evil man."

I refrained from asking what she had thought of Sébastien; I suspected her assessment might not be so kind. What I really wanted to ask her was more about herself, but before I could think of a specific question, the back door opened and Daniel came in, followed by Ben. "Found him," Daniel announced, unnecessarily.

"There you are, darling," Ben said, taking a moment to kick off his muddy boots before joining us at the table. "I'd have come to fetch you myself, but Dad and me have been fixing a leak in the carriage house roof. With a bit more work it'll make a proper little cottage for Claire, so she needn't keep sleeping on her friends' sofas in town. Well, unless she's in no fit state to drive," he added, chuckling as he ruffled his daughter's hair. "Colleen's still doing some painting. Claire, go and help your mum finish up, will you? Your gran and I will get Heather settled."

It was clear that Claire was being dismissed, and I wondered why. "We'll say goodnight too, son," Molly announced, before collecting a fresh cup and saucer and setting them in front of Ben. "Heather, we've put you in the blue room, in the attic. There's towels in the cupboard, and extra blankets if you need them, though I don't think it's to be too cold tonight. I'll see you in the morning."

I thanked her again, and bid her and Daniel goodnight, then watched as Ben collected his thoughts. "I'm not used to having a fortnight at loose ends this time of year," he said eventually, pouring himself a cup of tea and adding two sugars. "Winter, yes. But usually the autumn is one of the busiest times. Tara was a bit of a shock. I expect Claire told you?"

"She told me that the… the power wasn't what it should have been. Something about a motorway? And that Eric left, obviously."

Ben sighed, the creases deepening on his forehead. "I hope his dad's alright. Eric may have my blood, but John Heyward had the bringing up of him and he's got the right to the title," he added, though I hadn't questioned it. Perhaps others had: I already knew from personal experience that the magicians put great stock in bloodlines. "And all this has made me think of Anne again, for the first time in a long time. It wasn't meant to be, her and I, but she was a lovely girl." He shook his head and took a swig of his tea. "He'll be glad to see you've come, anyway, whenever he makes it back. You'll stay here till we travel again?"

It was a question out of courtesy, I thought; it was clear what answer he expected. "Well, if I won't be in the way," I said. "After all, how would I know how to find you guys again?"

He waved that away. "I'd tell you the next ten places we're to go, if it came to that. I'm not supposed to, of course. They've only just started letting me in on these things, myself!" he added, laughing. "There's not many places I still count as a youngster, but now that Mum and Dad only travel with us once in a while, they need me to stand in."

"Was that why you sent Claire out? Because you were prepared to tell me the next ten places you're going?"

"Well, better safe than sorry." He shrugged. "Besides, we're fixing that cottage for her, so she'd best have a hand in the work."

"And so... normally, when would she – would anybody – find out where you guys are going? When you get there?"

Ben laughed. "We're not quite so cryptic as that. And the longer someone is with us, the more they'll start to get the rhythm of things and have an idea what to expect. But usually? Most of us know when and where we're going next, and that's that. If we know someone will be away, they may get to know more; I made sure Eric knows our plans up till Christmas, though as you can see with Tara, things can change – and I certainly hope he's back before then. If not, he knows how to get in touch; I've only just given in to having one of those little pocket phones myself. Eric will always have a way to find us, don't worry."

After a pause, I asked the question he had left hanging. "Well, then: where are we going next? And when?"

CHAPTER FOUR

I awoke the next morning in a pale-blue room, ceiling slanting down almost to meet the floor on one side, watery light filtering in from a dormer window; it took me a solid minute or two to remember where I was, and that the previous day had not all been a dream. It would not have been too much of a stretch to think it had been – after all, some variation on the theme of searching in vain for the magicians had haunted my nights almost since I'd gotten home from Scotland.

But no, I was in an attic bedroom at Fernwood, the house guest of Ben's parents until such time as we decamped for a Belgian village called Wéris in two weeks' time. There were megaliths there – standing stones, and dolmens, Ben had said – and though the force there would be strongest in early November we were deliberately avoiding the peak. "Some things are beyond our needs, and what we want to be meddling with," he had told me the night before. "You'll find they're all different." He had also assured me that, despite my magical talent being in its infancy – and my complete lack of practice during my time back home in Canada – I would be able to be a contributing member of the group by that time. I couldn't quite imagine how, but I tried to take his word for it.

The day's events had left me so tired that I'd barely taken notice of any of my surroundings after leaving the kitchen. In the morning light, though, I could see that the house was indeed quite large. There seemed to be one other bedroom in the attic, and after going down the narrow stair I counted four doors in the upstairs hallway. The main staircase was broader, and led down to the front hall. Through open doors I spotted the living room on one side and what looked like a library on the other, but all the signs of life were coming from the kitchen. I suspected that it was the room where most of the action would be on any given day.

Colleen was at the stove, Claire sat at the table with a coffee and a small plate of eggs, and Ben was on the phone. "Yes, she's here." He was speaking loudly, as if on a bad connection. "Got here yesterday… Yeah…. Right, at Fernwood. Can you? That's brilliant… Well, when you get in, ring us – actually, ring Claire on her mobile – do you have it? Good – yeah, and she can come pick you up at the airport… Right. Right, excellent. See you soon."

For a moment, I thought he might be speaking to Eric, but he concluded with *Au revoir*; it had to be someone else. Thankfully, he spared me further wondering. "Aha, speak of the devil," he said, replacing the handset. "That was Manon – did you meet her? I don't think you did."

"She's very accomplished," Colleen added, tipping a slightly messy omelet onto a plate. "You probably saw her, even if you didn't meet. Her favourite trick is to make music with fire. I didn't think we'd see her until Wéris; she lives in Bruges."

I did remember seeing her act, at Callanish, though she herself had stood veiled in the darkness between bursts of flame; I doubted I would recognize her out of context. "Why is she coming here, then?"

All three of them looked at me as though I had missed something obvious, and Ben patted me on the shoulder. "She's coming to train you up, darling."

I spent one quiet day at Fernwood, exploring the grounds. The farm was tucked up against a forested hill, with grazing lands on either side. Despite the numbers of sheep that ambled about in the fields, I did not see a barn anywhere; Daniel explained that they'd never kept livestock themselves, being away too much of the year. "We rent out the grazing; some of the neighbour farms have given land over to forestry, so it works out," he told me, patting a woolly flank as we walked past. "Trees might bring in more money for us, but I prefer the view."

Looking out over the patchwork of fields and trees, I had to agree. "Claire told me that you'd fixed the place up quite a bit."

Daniel nodded. "It was laying vacant and we had it for a song, but it was damn near ruined. Hard times, then, and some people had just walked away from places like these. The roof had been leaking so long that the attic floor had just about rotted clean away, and the whole place was full of mould. The first few years we just pulled up a caravan in the garden and worked away at the place in between travelling, with the kids playing under our feet. Ben used to run and fetch my tools and things for me, being the eldest."

"I didn't know Ben had any siblings."

The old man sighed. "Aye. Nora, his sister – she married a fellow, a nice regular man, not one of us, and they moved to America. Said she wanted a 'normal life'. She's too frail to visit, now, though she's only just eighty-four; she was a good magician, but I suppose when she stopped, it couldn't help her much anymore. She has a fine son, and three grandchildren, and even a great-grand now, a baby. Imagine, seeing a fifth generation!"

Something in his eyes looked almost mournful, though. "Do you get to see them much?" I asked.

"Well, there's the thing, you see. After a point, how do you explain that your great-great-grandda is still kicking about?" He shook his head. "The longer time goes on, magic becomes the only explanation left, and if you don't want to speak of that anymore? No. Nora keeps us up with their news, and photos and such. We send gifts, but just sign them with our names, and let them think what they will – that we're some old uncle and auntie back in Ireland, I suppose."

"I'm sorry."

"No, don't be too sorry, my dear. All a parent can truly ask is for their children to be well and happy, and our Nora has been, even if not the way we once might have hoped. And we saw her, and her boy, come back often enough – as often as we would have if I'd been a normal man born in eighteen-ninety, for certain." Daniel exhaled heavily, but then smiled. "And Ben's hardly left our side, all these years, so how can I complain? Granted, we thought we might have lost him too, at one point."

This part of the story, I did know. "When he met Eric's mother." He had nearly left the magicians for her, a young nurse from Buffalo, New York.

"Just so. She was lovely – we met her, just the once – but since she wouldn't join us, we were well relieved when they went their separate ways. We'd had no idea, of course, that the poor girl was in the family way, or I would have made sure he did the right thing."

"But then he met Colleen."

"Oh, years later, though," he replied. "She's only about ten years older than Eric, truth be told."

I had wondered, I had to admit. "Daniel, can I ask you a question? Because I think – Colleen's family were magicians, right? She grew up with this?" When he nodded, I carried on. "And I get that when magic keeps you young – or whatever it does – I guess that age just matters less. But wouldn't Ben have known her when she was a little child? Wouldn't that make it… weird?"

Daniel was silent for a few seconds, just long enough that I worried the question had been offensive. "It's a fair thing to ask, especially when we're a small enough group. You'll have noticed that you don't see many children – at least, not our children – running about at the nightly shows? The kids are kept mostly to themselves – not in a bad way, but they don't get to know many adults outside of their family, and sometimes a teacher when there's enough kids to warrant one, till they're grown. It's partly that we're just a little old-fashioned, I suppose, but partly because of what you just asked. We're a small group, as I said, and if one's got a mind to marry and have a family, it's either go off with an outsider, as Nora did, convince them to join us – which does happen, now and then, but it's no easy feat – or marry a magician. It's best that we get to know each other as adults."

"Thanks. I'm sorry, I know it was a nosy question."

"Well, now you're with us, you've a right to understand how things work. Manon will see to it that you learn how to use your gifts, but there's plenty else you'll want to know. Never be afraid of asking questions, my dear."

CHAPTER FIVE

The next day, Claire was dispatched to Dublin to pick up Manon. By mid-morning, the car returned, and out of the passenger side stepped a woman who looked more like she was on her way to a Parisian café than an Irish farm. Manon was tall and angular, with impeccably-tailored clothes, not a hair out of place, little if any makeup, and the sort of striking facial features that made it hard to decide if she was beautiful or rather ugly. I could easily imagine her featuring in some kind of artistic street photography from the nineteen-sixties. Though I did not recognize her, it was clear from the first moment that she knew who I was.

"Bonjour," she said, kissing me on both cheeks, then holding my gaze for a moment. "Yes. I think there is much that I can teach you. Come."

She headed inside, apparently leaving Claire to deal with her baggage. Claire and I exchanged bemused looks, then I followed Manon in.

"You may wonder why they have asked me to come," she began, almost before I had gotten in the door of the library.

I raised one eyebrow at her businesslike, almost brusque tone. "I'd assumed it was because Ben and Eric didn't make much headway with me," I said, leaning on the door frame, arms crossed.

We regarded each other, for all the world like a principal and a student called to the office, before her posture softened. "Sit, please." Gesturing to one of the wing chairs, she sat down herself. "The training I can offer you will be difficult, and most novices have moments of resentment towards me during the process, but there is no need to start out on a bad footing. I am the one who they call upon when a magician joins us as an adult, as I walked that road myself. And yes," she continued, before I could ask, "your friend Eric apprenticed with me as well."

"Does this happen often?" I asked, settling in somewhat.

"Perhaps that answer depends on the scale by which you measure your time. There have been two others after Eric, and before yourself. But I believe you are already aware that this is not such a common experience – particularly in a case such as yours. It was Aurelia, who taught me."

The name meant nothing to me. If anything, part of me had expected her to cite Sébastien as her mentor, given the weight his name seemed to carry in magical circles. I filed the fact away, to be pondered later.

"My methods are considerably more modern than hers, of course," Manon resumed. "And I will set you to some tasks that may not seem related to magic at all. First, though, I must determine the skills you already possess. Tell me of your education."

We ran through my background – not just my degree, and my work history, but what languages I could get by in, where I had travelled, my opinion of religion and how I had found my way to the magicians. Manon queried me on my experience of martial arts – limited to one series of Tai Chi classes at the university rec centre

26

– and my familiarity with classic literature, along with numerous other topics, each seemingly more random than the last. Finally, just when I was nearly beginning to lose sight of the point of the interview, she asked me to show her some magic.

"Any magic?" I asked.

Manon shrugged. "Any that you can do. It will likely not be much."

She was right, of course. After nearly a month without practice, all I could manage after a few minutes of concentration was a trickle of water from my palms. If Manon was disappointed, or impressed, or completely indifferent, her expression did not betray it. She simply nodded, and told me to meet her in the back garden in twenty minutes' time.

"Oh yes," she added. "And wear something in which you can move."

Thus began one of the most exhausting – and baffling – fortnights I had ever experienced. Beginning at noon on that first day, and at dawn on the subsequent ones, Manon put me through the paces of all manner of tasks, all of them seemingly unrelated to each other and many that appeared to have no relationship to magic whatsoever. The entirety of the first afternoon was taken up with physical exercises, ranging from yoga to breakfalls on the rough, uneven lawn. The second day commenced with memory drills; at first she would arrange small items on a tray and test my recall after covering them with a cloth. By the third day, she was instructing me to memorize and recite, in order, all the book titles on a shelf of her choosing in the library. The shelves were not small; I was beginning to see why she had predicted her methods might inspire some resentment.

Eventually, as my stomach grumbled at the smell of dinner coming from the kitchen and I thought we must be nearly done for

the day, she began to quote passages in some unknown language –
or maybe complete bullshit that she just made up, I briefly thought – and
had me repeat them several times, until I could say them back in
any order and with precisely the intonation she had used.

"It is enough," she said at last. "We will be expected at the
dinner table."

I was just on the point of opening my mouth to ask what that
last bunch of gibberish had been all about, when she cracked the
first small hint of a smile I had seen all day. "Rest, and think on it,
and you will start to see what we are working towards."

Manon did not eat with the rest of us; Colleen took a tray to
her in her room. "She'll be worn out," Molly commented. "It's a
lot of training in not very much time."

"What about me?" I protested.

Ben, sitting on my left, just patted my arm before spearing
another forkful of food. "It's a lot to take on, and no mistake," he
said, through a mouthful of ham. "But you're made of strong
stuff."

Returning to the kitchen, Colleen shot him a look. "This is
what you could call a crash course; it'll be exhausting for both
student and teacher. Normally kids apprentice before graduating
into the show, usually for a year or so."

"Six months for me," Claire put in, sounding just slightly
smug. "Before I went to uni."

"But you didn't apprentice with Manon," I replied.

She shook her head. "No, she just works with incomers. I
trained with Jeannie Mac."

"Jeannie MacLennan," Colleen expanded. "You won't have
met her. She rarely performs; she's found her calling in being in

charge of educating the children. Mostly in what you'd think of as regular schooling, but she'll take an apprentice now and then. She runs a good school, on both counts."

Claire nodded. "Taught me most of my magic, AND got me into Trinity College Dublin without ever having set foot in a regular classroom. She's fantastic."

"And the kids don't really get to know the other adults, apart from their family and this Jeannie Mac?" I asked, thinking of what Daniel had told me.

"Not till they're sixteen or so," Ben said. "It's a bit like…"

"Debutantes?" I offered.

Claire seemed to find this hilarious, but Ben nodded. "Not so fancy, of course…"

"I'm sorry, Dad," Claire wheezed, "but I'm just after picturing Luke in a ball gown."

"Not so fancy," Ben repeated, rolling his eyes at his daughter. "But it's as good a comparison as any. It's a bit old-fashioned, but it's been working for us for a good long time."

"As I was saying." Colleen gave the words just a bit of an edge, hushing her family. "The kids apprentice for several months, sometimes longer. Adults joining us have it a little tougher, because you haven't grown up with it, but on the other hand you have some experience of the world on your side. How long they train depends a bit on how quickly they pick it up. Sometimes a month, sometimes half a year."

"And I've got two weeks."

Ben made a vague hand gesture. "You're not starting completely from scratch, after all. You joined us at the standing stones, and you'd taught yourself a fair bit. And, well…" Trailing off, he touched my forehead with one finger. I took his meaning: it was an echo of the gesture Raffaele had used in giving me his dying

29

blessing, as well as that of Sébastien, his mentor and my ancestor. Still an uncomfortable memory, but I had to acknowledge that the first signs of my own ability to use magic – at least, any signs that I had been able to see - all post-dated that moment. "Two weeks is a tall order," he resumed. "But if Manon thought you weren't up to it, she'd have turned on her heel and gone straight back to Belgium. She's no fool, and nor are you. You'll still have years of practice ahead of you – I'm still learning, myself, and I'm coming within spitting distance of ninety – but if you feel up to jumping in at Wéris, that'll be as good an education as any. Learn on the job, as they say. I've no doubt you'll be ready to play your part."

It was comforting to have a vote of confidence. With their assurances uppermost in my mind, I headed to bed not long after dinner was finished, not knowing what new trials the next day might bring. It was as I was lying in bed, just on the cusp of drifting off to sleep, that it hit me. *Magic words.*

Magic words – could that be what all the verbal nonsense had been about? It sounded absurd, even in my own head, but it was far from the strangest idea I had encountered. I pushed back the covers and stood in the middle of the room in my pajamas and bare feet. Holding my hands out, focusing, I chose a phrase at random and intoned it, just as Manon had instructed.

At first, I thought that nothing was happening, but I took a deep breath and repeated the words. This time, my hands began to tremble, feeling as though there was some kind of magnetic repulsion preventing me from moving them any closer together. It was like holding a slightly squishy ball between my palms. As I tried to press in against it, I saw a faint glow of blue light at the centre; pressing a little harder, though it strained my forearms and wrists to do so, made the light shine brighter, and closer to white.

I had thought I could only work magic with water. What other kinds of verbal commands were there, and what did they mean?

How could I go from this – or the water, for that matter – into something like the artistic spectacle that I had seen in the Menagerie, or in Claire's tent, or Eric's? That last thought seemed to finally stretch my concentration too far; the light and force vanished, leaving me with a dull ache radiating from my wrists to my shoulders.

Enough for one day, perhaps.

CHAPTER SIX

"So what do those words mean?" It was my first question at dawn the next morning.

Manon nodded. "They bring results, no?"

She hadn't answered my question, but I supposed that wasn't really the point. "But I went through almost every tent at Callanish – including yours, as it happens – and I never once saw anyone speaking as part of their performance." It was only in saying it that I realized that perhaps that wasn't strictly accurate – hadn't Sofia said something unintelligible when examining my fortune? I felt that she had, but certainly, most appearances from the magicians had not involved any sort of incantations as part of their work.

"You will remember that there were tents where you did not see any performer. Set pieces, one might say. To create a scene by magic and walk away, leaving it to amuse and delight for hours – this is more difficult, and requires some skill to fix. If you attain this level – it is not for everyone – you will need to develop your own words. A shorthand, if you will, for the hours of work it takes to first make such a creation. The words I have taught you, they are... examples. To illustrate the principle. But today, we will not be working with words. I will blindfold you now."

The magic words had proven their point; I bit back further questions and submitted to having a length of black cloth fastened over my eyes. There followed what seemed like an interminable series of random instructions: point north-east, stand on one foot in tree pose, draw various figures in the air with my dominant hand, and with the other, and then with each foot. Walking around the yard according to Manon's directions, having to feel out each step gingerly, wary of unseen hazards on the rough ground. After a couple of hours of this nonsense, I stopped and, still blindfolded, kicked off my shoes and socks. It was cold and damp, to be sure, but I felt in better contact with the ground when I was able to sense the textures under my toes.

"Twenty paces north, and faster," Manon instructed.

Which way is north? There was no point in asking the question aloud; I knew I would not receive an answer. I tried thinking back through the sequence of motions I had been through since the blindfold had been put on, but I could not have said with any confidence what direction I was facing even if I could look around. I would have to figure it out another way.

It occurred to me that this was the point of the whole exercise.

Planting my feet more solidly on the ground, even digging into the grass a bit with my toes, I tried to sense it, to reach out for the answer with my mind. I remembered the energy pouring out of the stones at Callanish, and the fainter echo at Tara. That had to come from somewhere, did it not? I was beginning to feel like I was rooted to the spot, though in truth I had only stood there a few seconds. A communication between my soles and the soil, like a tree drawing water up from underground. And then, without consciously considering the matter any further, I took slightly less than a quarter-turn to my right, and strode forward twenty steps with as much speed as I dared: hardly running for a bus, but definitely less cautious than I had been before.

When my feet were still again, I heard Manon's voice. "Take the blindfold off."

Wondering whether I had done something right, or something quite wrong, I fumbled with the knot and tugged it off. "Well?"

She was standing some distance behind me: about twenty paces, in fact. When I looked more closely, I could just make out the trail of my footprints in the damp grass. Manon was standing where I had started. "See for yourself. Leave the blindfold where you now stand."

I dropped it, marking my place, and returned to the starting point. She handed me a compass. "North-northeast," I announced, comparing my trajectory to that of the needle. "Close, but no cigar."

"You are hard on yourself." She took the compass back from me. "Society now says that this is a bad thing, but I disagree. For a magician, new or old, it is a very good thing indeed. You may wish to put your shoes back on; the temperature will soon begin to drop."

As I was pulling on my left sock, I saw Claire come around the corner of the house. "Sorry to interrupt, but will you be wanting any lunch? Gran's asking."

Was it that time already? About to look to Manon – for what? Permission? – I changed my mind and answered for myself. "Well, I think we've just finished one thing here. I could do with a quick bite of something."

"I will eat at some time later," Manon said. "Our next activity will require me to set up some components."

Apparently dismissed, I stuck my feet into my shoes and followed Claire inside. "When you did your apprenticeship, or training, or whatever, did you have to do this many things that had nothing to do with magic?" I asked, once I assumed we were out of earshot.

"Oh, like you wouldn't believe," she replied, with a hint of a laugh. "Tumbling, yoga, pushups, the whole bit. The worst were the posture exercises. Jeannie Mac would have me stand at attention with a book on my head for a half-hour at a time, some days. I still do the yoga, but the rest of it..." She shook her head.

"Why, though? I'd have thought that learning to be a magician would be more about concentration and focus and that sort of thing. When she had me doing memorization yesterday, at least that made a little more sense."

Claire shrugged and held the kitchen door open for me. "Well, that's the thing, isn't it? Everybody thinks it's about being really smart and doing everything with your mind. It's about the body. Making the mind and body work together. People live in their heads all the time, and don't even know their bodies, no matter how much they look at themselves in the mirror. But the better you can work with your body – in whatever ways you can – the better you can work with your magic. It bloody sucks sometimes, but there it is."

After lunch, I found that Manon's prediction had indeed come to pass; a sharp east wind had blown up, and the temperature had taken a more autumnal turn. "We will work inside," she announced, although I suspected it might be less to do with our comfort and more to do with the wind threatening to blow away the length of silk in her hands. In the library, she spread the fabric out over one of the armchairs like a too-small dustcover; it was a dusty pink colour that I found quite ugly, and I wondered what I was going to be expected to do with it.

"Utility magic," she told me. "This is what we will work on for the next days."

That sounded more like it, even if the words 'utility' and 'magic' seemed like strange bedfellows. "What sort of utility?"

She blinked at me. "The carnival. You of course realize that there is far more work than just the pretty showpieces. And do not mistake me, much of it is work, of the most mundane kind – and none among us are above putting our hands to it."

"Of course." I had wondered, in Scotland, how things got done – the tents, the food – and how much of it was aided by magic. For once, it seemed I was actually going to get an answer.

"There are many skills needed, and ways in which magic can be put to use to serve our ends. When we arrive at Wéris, you will see where your skills may be put to use. Today, we will see what your skills are. Begin by changing the silk."

It was obvious that I was to change it by magic – and that I was being thrown in at the deep end. As much as I hated to have to ask questions, I spoke up. "Change what, exactly?"

Manon shrugged, apparently uncaring. "Anything you like. More precisely, anything you can. I shall take my luncheon now."

She left me to it, which I had to admit was something of a relief. After a while, I managed to produce a little current of air that stirred the edges of the fabric – satisfying enough for a novice like me, but it did not actually alter anything about the piece of cloth. Picking it up off the chair, I examined it more closely. It was fine fabric, apart from the unfortunate colour. Letting it drape over my hand, I was reminded of the magicians' tents. How did they set up so many tents, so quickly? It had to be magic.

And where did they store all those tents, anyhow? Would it not be easier to travel around with a trunk full of swatches hardly larger than placemats? "If it's a tent they want, it's a tent they'll get," I muttered, just barely aloud. "And maybe not a damn pink one, while I'm at it."

By the time the wind had died down outside, I had dredged up every bit of energy I possessed, plus a little that might have come from elsewhere. My hands were shaking, I was dehydrated, and I had the beginnings of a monster headache. But the silk covered the whole of the chair, with excess fabric pooling on the floor. Not big enough for a magician's tent, granted – perhaps a play tent for a magician's child – but an order of magnitude larger than the size it had started out. And although it had not been my express intent, something subconscious must have worked its way into my barely-understood magic, because the silk was no longer the same sickly greyish-rose, but a deep raspberry colour. Gingerly, half-afraid it might disappear like the tiger I had met once in the Menagerie, I picked up a fold of the cloth between my fingers. The texture was maybe just a bit rougher than I remembered, but it was silk, all right. Tugging at the fabric, I could not tear or warp it. Satisfied, I let it fall again, and left the room. Whatever else Manon might have in mind, I was doing nothing else until I had a cup of tea.

No one was in the kitchen, but Colleen had shown me how to use the big Aga stove to boil the kettle, and where the tea was kept. I had just sat down to wait for the pot to brew when I heard an exclamation from the hallway. A moment later, Claire popped her head into the kitchen. "Was that you? The silk square test?"

"I didn't know it was a test." I supposed all of it was a test, in one way or the other. Although I'd been formally accepted into the group, I would still have to prove myself, probably for quite some time to come.

"Well, nicely done. She's standing in there, just staring at it. I have a feeling you may have just earned yourself some harder lessons, though."

Claire wasn't wrong. Over the next few days, we went over virtually every kind of conjuring that was used in holding the show together. My favourite was the food, because it answered a question I had wondered about since my first visit. I had had a hard time imagining the magicians toiling in a kitchen - not to mention grocery shopping – to produce the laden feast tables or circulating trays of treats that had been in evidence in Scotland, but then again, the food had been no illusion. The truth was, it was a little of both: magic and hard work. Not that the magic was easy in any case, but Manon drilled me over and over until I was able to turn a small pot of soup into enough for an army, or produce a bottomless pot of tea. And then there was the marking of sigils, used on the hands of visitors as they entered – far more elegant than ink – and the shields that could hide an entrance, or even a whole tent, from a casual glance. I marveled at the fact that the magicians' carnival had at least as much, if not more, sorcery behind the scenes as there was on display.

On the thirteenth day, I came down in my workout clothes at dawn once again and found Manon standing in the front hall with her suitcase. "I return to Bruges today," she announced. "There are matters I must attend to before we go to Wéris."

"Are we done, then?"

"We are, though you are not." For the first time in all our days of training together, she gave a genuine smile. "Your education will continue: through observation, through practice, and when you are ready you will take a journey of discovery. You show promise, Heather Ross, but you must continue to be hard on yourself. And remember: not all the lessons come from magic, so do not discount the knowledge earned in your former life." She took a step closer and lowered her tone. "And continue to be wise in your choice of friends."

A taxi pulled up at the door; I wondered at her calling for one all the way out in the countryside, when Claire or Ben or Colleen could have easily driven her to Dublin. "I will see all of you at Wéris." Kissing both my cheeks as she had on our first meeting, she picked up her case, stepped into the cab, and was gone.

I expected the family to react to Manon's departure with surprise, but the news barely earned a raised eyebrow. "She's not much of one for hanging about," Ben said. "And besides, I'm sure you could use a day's rest before we travel. There'll be plenty to do once we get there, after all."

"If nothing else, I should probably try to re-acclimatize myself to the late nights," I replied, sitting down to join them at the breakfast table.

"Oh, that only takes a day." He passed the teapot down to me. "That reminds me: do you mind staying with Claire and some of the other young folks while we're there? We've a friend in the village who has an old coach house fixed up with bunks; she prefers to just have women stay, so usually a bunch of the single girls kip there. It's a bit basic, but it'd give you a chance to get to know some more people."

I took a moment to finish my mouthful. "I'm not one to turn up my nose at hospitality, if they'll have me. I'm sure it'll be fine." Once again, I was mostly just pleased to still be classed in with the young people at the age of thirty-eight. "How long will we stay at Wéris?" I added, testing out the unfamiliar feel of the name.

"Not as long as Callanish. I can't say for sure, but I'd guess ten days, maybe a fortnight at the outside."

"How do you want to get down there, Heather?" Claire asked, taking a slice of toast and adding more butter to it.

"Um, I don't know," I replied, unsure of what my choices were.

"Ben and I are going to fly to Brussels, and take the train from there," Colleen said. "Arthur and Sarah…"

"Luke's mum and dad," Claire supplied.

"Yes. Arthur and Sarah will meet us in Brussels and we'll go on together. Perhaps some of the others will as well. Claire's taking the scenic route."

Claire grinned. "I'm making a proper road trip of it, like you do in America."

"Canada."

She waved a hand. "Whatever. I'm taking the car and ferry over to connect with Eleanor – she's got one of the vans – and then we'll drive down and pick up a few others along the way."

"And spending the night in London has nothing to do with this plan," Colleen added, prompting her daughter to roll her eyes.

"Mum, I'm a grown woman and I lived on my own for over five years, between uni and working. Honestly. London is halfway, and we can stay in Rickmansworth with Tom's family. It's not like we're going to drive thirteen or fourteen hours straight through. You should come with us, Heather," she said, turning to me. "It'll be way more fun than flying down. And Mum will think you're keeping me out of trouble." Laughing, she made a face at her parents.

"Well, if you put it like that, how can I refuse?" I replied. In truth, Claire's plan did sound like more fun, and I was curious to meet more of the 'young people' – though for all I knew, some of them might well be older than me – and continue to find my way into this strange little community.

"There's just one thing," she said. "Are you up for leaving this afternoon? We could wait and go at the crack of dawn tomorrow for the early ferry, but this way we could stop off tonight at Eleanor's."

"Sure, why not?"

I spent the rest of the morning repacking my clothes and the assorted other things I had seen fit to bring with me - funny to be living out of a backpack for the foreseeable future – until there was a knock at the door. Molly was waiting there. "Can I come in, love?" She looked at my bag and the few odds and ends that I had not yet put in. "I hope it's not too hard for you, being on your own," she said, sitting down on the straight-backed chair by the dormer window. "I know it was Eric that particularly asked you to join us. We were so disappointed when he had to go back to America so suddenly. Daniel and I don't get to see him as often as we'd like."

"Because of Colleen?"

Molly sighed. "I'm sure it must seem terribly harsh, and she doesn't mean to be."

I sat down on the edge of the bed. "I guess it must have been quite a shock, when he showed up."

"And she never quite got past it. It doesn't help that Eric's just about the spitting image of Ben as a young man. He really looks far more like his father than Claire does. Heaven's sakes, is that the time?" she added, glancing at the old alarm clock ticking away in the corner. "I should let you get on, my dear. What I really wanted to come up and say was, that you are welcome back in this house any time you'd like. The auld man and I have been delighted to have you here, just delighted. And we know you'll do great things. Great things."

CHAPTER SEVEN

Claire and I didn't talk much on the drive to Dublin; we would be cutting it close on time to make the ferry, so her focus stayed on the road as she exceeded several speed limits on our way to the terminal. Thankfully, we made it with a few minutes to spare, and had nearly two hours of sailing ahead of us to pass at our leisure.

"Have you been to Wéris before?" I asked, once we had settled into a pair of chairs in the cafeteria.

She took a sip of her coffee and looked at the rain pattering against the windows. "Sort of. I've been there, but not in the way you mean." Looking around, she checked that there was no one within earshot before continuing. "I was there a couple of times when I was a kid, but it was before I was performing. The village is a sweet little place, and Jeannie Mac took us round to see some of the stones, but only during the daytime."

Thinking back, I definitely remembered having seen one or two families with children present on the night of the lunar event on Lewis, and said so.

"They're all different," she explained. "The places, I mean. We're at Callanish so rarely, and what happens there is so strange. It's a bit of a special case. And the kids were just spectators."

"Growing up like you did…" I tried to think of how to phrase the question. "Your dad's already told me how the kids get kind of sheltered from the rest of the group till they're older. How much exposure did you have to the… I hate to say it, but - the real world?"

"For me, or for the kids in general?"

"I don't know," I replied. "Either."

She shrugged. "I guess it's like anything; it kind of depends on the parents. My mum and dad were big believers that I should be prepared to have whatever kind of life I wanted, so even though they never let me go to school when I went through my phase of asking to go, they made sure I had at least some things that a regular girl my age would have. TV, books, we went to the cinema when we weren't travelling, that sort of thing. We'd go to the village funfair if we were home at the time. I had a couple of pen pals in America and Japan, once I was old enough that Mum trusted me not to blab about magic."

"Real pen pals?" I asked, briefly diverted. "I wouldn't have thought someone your age would still write actual letters."

"Most people my age don't have a dad born in the nineteen-twenties, right? The internet was one thing that kind of passed me by till pretty recently; we never had it at home until I was starting to think about uni and Jeannie Mac told Mum and Dad I might have to do some distance courses to qualify for my leaving certificate. And it was exciting when we'd be on the road and I could collect postcards to mail off to my friends – I could never say why we travelled so much, but they just thought I was so lucky, not to have to go to school."

There was a long pause. I had just about decided on going up to the counter for another tea, when Claire spoke again. "I used to write letters to Eric, too. In the winter when we'd be at home for a couple of months at a time. When I was small, I never quite knew who he was to us. When we were with the troupe, he'd come around to see me, so I knew he had to be family, or as good as, since those were the only magicians I'd spend time with, as a kid – but he only ever came to Fernwood once or twice, and never stayed. I know why now, of course, but it was puzzling at the time."

"When did you find out?"

She pursed her lips and looked up at the ceiling for a second or two. "I think I was… eleven, or maybe twelve? It was one of the few times Eric came to the house. Mum and I had been in town, at a film, and came home to find him talking with Dad in the library. I was thrilled, and asked if he could stay. I don't think I'd ever seen him and Mum in the same room before, so it was the first time I noticed how she is around him. You've seen it, I think: she's not outright rude, but she's frosty. It was awkward. He just got up and said he didn't think it was a good idea, and that he'd see me soon, and left. After that – well, I got in a bit of a strop with my mum. I blamed her for being mean to him. You know what it's like when you're that age: everything is black and white." About to drink more coffee, she looked into the cup and found it empty. "Well, that night Dad came up to my room and said we needed to have a talk, and he told me the story. Of course, at that age, as an only child, finding out I actually had a half-brother was just about the most exciting thing that had ever happened."

"I can imagine."

"I mean, it's not the same as having a real sibling, in a way," she continued. "As much as he was around for me growing up, and he's always looked out for me – still does – but the age difference is so huge. He would have been more like an uncle, even if there wasn't all the weirdness with Mum. And of course, he's got his own brother and sister, more like his own age, that he grew up with."

Eric had told me a fair bit about his parents' backstory, but not much about his life in Buffalo. After all, I had only known him for three weeks. "I guess technically they're his half-siblings too, but I can see how it's different. Although he's spent nearly half his life with you guys by now."

"True." She sighed. "I hope he gets back in time to catch up with us in Belgium. If not, Dad's probably told him a few more stops after that. Eric almost never misses a show, though; those couple of days at Tara felt very strange without him there."

Claire was starting to seem a bit melancholy, so I made an attempt to change the subject. "I guess you'll be the first to know once he's back, since he'll want his phone again. But tell me, who are we collecting on this road trip? I know we're staying with Eleanor tonight, and was it Tom tomorrow?"

She nodded, brightening up. "Eleanor lives in Chester. Have you ever been there? It's a bit precious, and full of tourists, but it's an interesting town. My first time joining the main show was there, so I've developed a bit of a soft spot for the place. And Eleanor: you probably wouldn't have run into her last time. She works behind the scenes, for the most part."

At that, something twigged: a passing mention that I had heard. "Doesn't she do something with jamming cellphones, or something like that? So that people can't record you – us – performing?"

"You're well-informed, indeed. Yeah. She was the latest to join us, before you, and she worked as some kind of computer security consultant before that. I guess it was a natural way to use her skills."

I wasn't sure yet whether I knew a natural way to apply my skills. At least the training with Manon had shown me that I had some.

After landing we had a rainy, hilly drive through North Wales before arriving in Chester, the heart of which was a black-and-white confection of genuine medieval buildings and Victorian-era Tudor revival. Eleanor had a flat above a print shop, a little outside the town centre.

Eleanor herself was short and plump, with dark hair that hung in heavy bangs over a pair of retro cat's-eye glasses. Any worries I might have had about imposing on her hospitality were put to rest immediately, and I found her remarkably chatty. Within half an hour I had learned that she had been a part of the troupe for seven years, and also occasionally joined in on an amateur burlesque revue in between travels with the magicians. "It's ironic, isn't it?" she asked, gesturing around at her apartment, which was decorated in a sort of mid-century thrift-shop pastiche. "I'm thirty-nine, have a degree in computer science and I'm hooked on the past, and now I hang around with a bunch of people who lived it and most of them are more modern than me. I never would have believed it."

"How did you wind up with them?" I asked.

"They came here," she said, "when I was a teenager. Obviously, I was hooked. I'd always dreamed of doing magic – taught myself some card tricks and stuff from when I was a kid, nothing really magical, but I was pretty good at sleight of hand. And, well… I've made my own niche in the world now, but my younger life was a pretty rough time for me. If they'd have had me then, I would have packed up and gone without so much as a second thought. Every time they came back around, I dropped everything and just tried to soak up as much of it as I could. And then seven years ago, I was performing – with the burlesque, that is - and I had a bit of 'magic' in my dance," she continued, putting exaggerated air quotes around the word. "A woman came up after the show and gave me her card. Not that unusual, though I was pleased it was a woman for a change, even if she was a little old for me. I didn't look at it till afterwards. But it was the magicians' card, of course – I expect you'll have seen one? – and the next night I found they'd come back to Chester. I asked for Manon, the woman whose name was on the card, and next thing I know I'm getting told that I'm a talented magician, a real one. I thought it was a complete scam at first, but of course, here I am! I got quizzed a lot about my family at first, but nobody's been able to figure out where I could have got it from, least of all me. Either somebody way back in the mists of time, or else I'm a freak of nature. I'm fine with the latter," she added, grinning and pulling out a bottle of red wine. "Drink?"

The next day started at the railway station, where we collected a man named Gavin who had a pronounced Scottish accent that I only heard a little of before he dozed off in the back seat. A couple of hours down the highway, we stopped off near Coventry and picked up Luke; I was delighted to see him again, and he made a point of declaring me as his 'cousin, or second cousin at least', to everyone else in the van. Mid-afternoon found us arriving at a tidy suburban row house on the outskirts of London, where I was introduced to Tom, who looked a bit flustered to have all these people descending on what was clearly his parents' home. I thought he was probably about Luke's age, give or take, and he seemed quite shy compared to the rest of the boisterous company. However, when we all took the Tube into the city and visited a few pubs, he opened up a bit. "I've heard about the Devil's Bed in Wéris," he said, lowering his voice a bit after he was shushed by Eleanor and Gavin. "They say Satan himself comes out and sits there," he continued, in a dramatic tone.

Luke set his pint glass down and leaned back on the bench. "For Christ's sake, do you hear yourself? Who told you that?"

Tom turned red, and muttered something I didn't hear.

Eleanor leaned in. "Leave him alone, Luke. I think we all know there's no such thing, but the truth is, neither of you have been there yet. Don't try to be experts on something you haven't seen for yourself."

Sunday morning we set our sights for the Channel Tunnel, where the van was loaded onto a train that took us through to France. By afternoon we were driving through the south-western part of Belgium, spirits running palpably higher the closer we got to our destination. It was such a strange contrast to my journey to the Isle of Lewis several weeks before, when I had not yet even been certain that the magicians would come – or my arrival at Tara expecting the magicians and finding none. I wondered if the people of Wéris cherished fond memories of past visits of this strange carnival, and how surprised they would be to see us again.

"Will there be a show tonight?" I asked, remembering again what day of the week it was.

Gavin shook his head. "No. Not everyone's going to be here yet. We'll get settled in – the lads and I at Gaetan's farm, and you ladies with Madame Virginie – and lay low till the rest arrive tomorrow. Then the fun begins."

CHAPTER EIGHT

We had been driving for some time along a country road thinly lined with grey-green trees, when Eleanor slowed down. "This is it, right?"

In the front passenger seat, Gavin agreed. "Rue des Combattants. See, there's the sign. Turn left."

We took a brief detour through the village – several dozen houses, a tiny museum and a couple of restaurants and guest houses – to drop off Luke, Gavin and Tom at a house just to the east of the town, then backtracked to where we would stay. My first impression of Wéris was that it was a cute little place, and very tidy. The houses were mostly two-story, a mix of eras and building materials but all in a similar architectural style, and most of them fronted directly onto the road without a yard or garden in between. I had no idea how populated the district might be, or what kind of audience to expect when the show opened the next night.

"That's quite a good spot," Eleanor said, pointing out a brasserie with a terrace opening onto what seemed to be the village square. "We'll meet up there tonight and see who else has made their way into town early."

We wound up at a grey stone house, the upper floor of which was half-timbered like the buildings I had seen in Chester. Adjoining the back corner of the house was an outbuilding that might have once been a compact barn. By the time we had parked the van, a woman was emerging from the side door of the house.

"Bonjour?" she said, sounding slightly hesitant until she spotted Eleanor. "Oh! It is you!" Quickening her pace, she came around the front of the van and embraced her, kissing her on both cheeks. "We had thought perhaps to see you earlier in the season. Will you all stay? How long? Do come in, come into the kitchen until I find the keys to the loft."

As we all retrieved our bags out of the back, I breathed a sigh of relief that her English was clearly excellent. Despite having had the several years of French instruction required by a Canadian education, my conversational command of the language was long since out of practice. Still, I mustered up what I could. "Merci pour votre hospitalité," I began, hoping I wasn't butchering it. "Je m'appelle Heather Ross, et je viens du Canada, mais mon Français est... comment est-ce qu'on dit 'rusty'?"

Our host was kind enough to smile at my clumsy attempt. "Rouillé," she replied. "But do not worry, I like to keep my English in use. I am Virginie Bertrand. Do come in." We followed her into a surprisingly streamlined kitchen. "No, no, leave your shoes, it is fine," Virginie instructed, though she kicked off her own boots. "I was just about to go to the garden, but it will wait. You must be the first to arrive. Will the circus be in the same place as before?"

As Eleanor did her best to field the rapid-fire questions, I looked around and tried to form a picture of our new friend. I guessed Virginie's age at somewhere in her late fifties, and her appearance was mildly bohemian, somewhat at odds with the spare, almost Spartan interior of her home. I glimpsed a grand piano through the doorway into what must be the living room, and a splash of colour from a massive abstract canvas hanging on the wall. Similar, though smaller, artworks hung above the kitchen counter where I would normally expect cabinets to be. But there were no photos or knick-knacks about, none of the sorts of things that might tell a story about someone's personality.

Eventually, after plying us with coffee from a gleaming espresso machine that took pride of place on the counter, Virginie showed us to the upper level of the barn. The stairs opened onto a large white room, floored with huge wood planks, probably original to the building, somewhat uneven but sanded and varnished to a golden glow. Six sets of sturdy-looking wooden bunk beds lined the walls, with small windows above the upper bunks letting in the afternoon light. "Since you are the first, you shall have the choice of your beds," she informed us. "Please come and go just as you like, but I prefer that you not bring gentlemen friends."

Considering that she was welcoming us to stay at the drop of a hat, her one rule seemed more than reasonable - even if I had had any ideas about 'gentlemen friends', which I most assuredly did not. The place brought back memories of youth hostels, albeit cleaner and nicer than most of the ones I had experienced. Although briefly tempted to take a top bunk, I opted for the bottom one opposite Eleanor's. "Surely she must rent this out to other travellers a lot of the time," I pointed out, after Virginie had left us to it. "Doesn't it ever happen that you turn up on the doorstep of someone like this and they can't put you up because they have other guests?"

Eleanor shrugged. "Usually it just seems to work out. Once in a while we have to change plans; usually we either find somewhere else to lay our hats, or if it's really dire we might just move on, or a few people go home. That almost never happens, though."

Once we had freshened up and settled in, Eleanor offered to take us on a walk around the megaliths, explaining that they were scattered in different directions around the village rather than grouped together as at Callanish. As we walked along the road, the sun was just starting to decline towards the west, casting a warm light that gilded the fields around us. The land was relatively flat, apart from a ridge of low forested hills extending off to the left. Our first destination, perhaps a ten-minute walk from Virginie's house via a shortcut across a field corner, was a small row of standing stones and a dolmen: a structure rather like a roofed box made of massive slabs of stone. It was a term I remembered from archaeology lectures, many years before, but seeing one in person was a different matter altogether. The monuments looked like the same grey stone that was used on the village homes; it must have been quarried somewhere in the area. I laid my palms on each of the stones in turn, as did Eleanor and Claire. Energy was definitely more present here than it had been at Tara, and quite unlike what I'd experienced at Callanish. The texture of these stones was different, rougher, and their energy seemed to take a similar tone, like the difference between violin and electric guitar.

"It feels… disorganized," Claire said, taking her hands away.

"They've been moved." Eleanor moved from one stone to the next, touching them gently. "Archaeologists found them knocked down in the fields about a hundred or so years ago and put them back in their original places. I took a tour from the little local museum the first time I came here," she added, by way of explanation. "I don't know if that's why they feel the way they do, but I've always thought that they were just slightly out of tune. You'll feel a difference on the dolmen; it's been disturbed, too, but not as much."

The dolmen was nearly as tall as me, and probably six feet wide by twenty feet long. Claire actually went inside it, but only for a moment. Across another field we found a similar grouping of stones. Finally, we struck out towards the hill to the south, off the road and up a hiking trail to what seemed to me the most impressive sight yet. At the crest of a ridge overlooking the village was a stone that stood nearly twice my height, reclining back at what looked like a precarious angle, and mostly coloured a streaky white. "Is this… painted?" I asked, as we got close to it.

"The villagers do it, at the equinox. It's chalk, I think," Eleanor said.

Claire perked up. "Oh! My dad told me about this. Isn't there a legend that this rock plugs the exit to hell, or something, and they colour it white to keep the devil inside?"

Eleanor nodded, rolling her eyes just a little. "So they say. There's also a rock at the bottom of the hill called the Devil's Bed. I don't believe in the devil for a second, but something about the energy there doesn't suit me. This place, though, is one of my favourites. It's called the Pierre Haina – I think it means 'stone of the ancestors'. It's actually part of the hill, not something that was brought here."

I was reluctant to touch the Pierre Haina, for fear of rubbing off the chalk that had been so recently redone, but I sat down quite close to it, overlooking the fields below. Joining me, Eleanor pointed out the rough location where she thought we would set up the tents the next night, then retrieved a water bottle and a few snacks from her bag, offering them to us.

"Do you mind if I go on ahead and look at the Devil's Bed?" Claire asked.

Eleanor pointed her in the right direction and said we'd catch up later, after which the two of us sat and ate our granola bars in companionable silence for a few minutes. "Can I ask you a question?" she said, eventually.

"Of course."

She turned to look at me, pushing her glasses up her nose. "Do you know what's up with Eric?"

Surprised, I told her that he'd had a family emergency back in the States. "I don't know too much apart from that. Why?"

"That's what I'd heard. I just wondered if there was any news. He'll be missed, if he doesn't get back in time to join us here. We have our share of drama, the lot of us, but he's one of the characters who just about everyone is fond of."

"Everyone but Colleen?" I asked.

"Well, there's that, of course," she said, waving my comment away. "And Stasia, obviously. Oh, they had a thing for a few years," she added, when she noticed my blank look. "Before my time. I gather it ended in fireworks on both sides, and not the good kind. But aside from them, I don't think he really realizes how well-liked he is, or how important he is to the group. Even though he's been here for years and years, I think he still sees himself as an outsider."

"Do you ever feel like that?" I knew I certainly did, but I hoped it would pass in a good deal less than twenty-five years.

Eleanor was taking a sip from her water bottle, and nearly did a spit-take. "Where do I even start? I'm kind of an outsider by trade. But here? No. This is home. A few of the older ones raised some eyebrows the one time I brought a girlfriend round, but all in all this lot have been far more accepting than just about anyone else. Certainly more so than my actual family. "

I considered her last statement, but it was clear from her tone that she was not inviting discussion on the topic. Instead, I asked another question that I had wondered about. "How come you don't perform? For an audience, I mean. It's clearly not stage fright."

"Oh, I do, once in a while," she said. "But a lot of what I do behind the scenes, it's stuff that no one else *can* do. And it's important. If people start posting pictures of us and filming performances and putting it online... it's not going to be the same any more. Even though the show's all magic, half the magic is in the mystery, you know? And besides, it's so much fun. Like a big logic puzzle." She shrugged. "This is a weird life, and for people like you and me who didn't grow up with it, there's no point in doing it if you're not having fun."

"Did you figure that out right away? What you wanted to do here, I mean."

She shook her head. "I did start helping out with it pretty much right off the bat, but at first I just assumed that it would be something I'd do on the side – like how we all help with the setup and teardown – and that I'd develop some kind of a performance as my main thing. It was a year or so, before I realized that the so-called side job was my favourite part of the whole business. Don't worry if it takes you a while to find your niche. Even if it feels like a few people are treating you like a special case because of the whole... well, the Sébastien thing. That drama will die down quickly enough," she added, waving it away. "It always does. I suspect Eric's absence is already taking over as the next big topic of conversation. Anyhow, shall we go catch up with Claire?"

We dusted ourselves off and started down the hill. The sun was noticeably lower, almost horizontal through the trees; we must have spent longer at the Pierre Haina than I'd realized. Passing by the Devil's Bed – a massive horizontal stone slab that did look for all the world like a bed with a headrest – it was clear that Claire had long since gone, so we continued on towards the village proper.

"There's one other thing, before we join the others," Eleanor said, as we made our way along the quiet roadside.

"What is it?"

She was looking at me as if trying to figure something out. "I'm not asking. I'm really not. But you should know, your name and Eric's have been getting mentioned a lot. In the same sentence, as it were."

"We're just friends," I said immediately. "Believe me. The ink's barely dry on my divorce papers – and after my ex..."

Eleanor held up both hands. "No explanations needed. I don't jump to conclusions. Just don't be surprised if some people do, especially the older ones."

I supposed that having everyone involved in my business was going to become an inevitable fact of life: something else that would take some getting used to after the anonymity of a big city. "People are just going to think what they're going to think," I concluded. "I can't be responsible for that."

"Good. Now for god's sake, let's go and get a bottle of wine."

The evening was still warm for the end of September and the terrace of the brasserie on the village square was nearly full. Many of the faces were familiar, even if I had yet to match them all with names; several people called greetings to Eleanor, and a few nodded and smiled at me as we passed. We found Claire at a table inside, a carafe of red wine already out as she glanced at the menu. In one corner, a table of people were chatting excitedly amongst themselves and taking it in turn to sneak looks out the window. I was too far away to tell what language they might be speaking – probably French – but I could guess the message: *The magicians have come.*

"There you are, cousin." Luke materialized at my elbow just as we were about to sit. "You've had the grand tour? Gav hiked us all over half the countryside, I think." Pulling up a chair, he slumped down in an exaggerated posture of exhaustion, while managing to also signal the waiter for more wineglasses. "I see some of the oldsters have already arrived."

Claire cuffed him round the side of the head. "Stop being such a smart-arse. Being the youngest one in the show is nothing to pat yourself on the back about. Have you decided yet whether you're doing your own tent this time? Luke's usually performed with his dad and uncle," she explained in an aside to me. "Callanish was his first time on his own."

"It was tougher than I expected," Luke added, dropping his clever front for a moment. "Once a night was plenty. I went back to Dad and Uncle Bill at Tara, not that we were there long. But I might give it a go again. Unless... what about you, Heather? Did you have anything planned yet?"

"Me?" I hadn't been expecting to contribute much to this particular line of conversation. "I figured I'd help out with food, or sell tickets or something. I've barely had any training, let alone a chance to start thinking about an act. I'd just be kind of making shit up."

Luke shrugged. "So? What do you think the rest of us are doing? This is perfect, then; you don't have to come up with something entirely on your own. Honestly, even if you just want to kind of help me out with mine, it's a good way to take a first stab at it. I thought you might've been working with Eric, but I hear he's still not back."

"I'm not working with anybody yet," I replied, ignoring the look that Eleanor directed my way.

"Well, then." Luke filled my glass. "What about it? I really could use the help - although if that goes beyond the four of us here at this table, I'll deny it to my dying day."

"If you put it like that." I could see he wasn't liable to take no for an answer. And there was merit in his suggestion; I might as well just go ahead and jump headlong into performing while my small amount of training was fresh, and before I could take too much time to get nervous about it. "We'd better figure something out before tomorrow night, then."

After dinner, Claire and Eleanor moved on to catch up with some of the other new arrivals, while Luke and I switched – at my insistence – from wine to strong black coffee, and started talking about how we could pool our talents. By the end of my first cup, we had an idea that seemed as though it just might work.

CHAPTER NINE

Walking through the village the next day, excitement was palpable in the air. People eyed me with frank curiosity: was I one of the magicians whose arrival was being whispered about? It was as clear as if they were to ask the question directly. I was on my way to meet Luke for a practice session when I bumped into Ben, just emerging from the front door of a whitewashed house. "There you are, darling. We've just arrived." He gave me a hug, and pressed something into my hand. "Give these out where you see fit, but not all at once, alright? I'm off to see the others about tonight. Is someone showing you where to go for setting things up?" he added.

"Eleanor's going to walk me over," I replied. "About five o'clock, right?"

Ben nodded. "See you then."

As he strode off down the street, I looked down at the small stack of magician's cards in my hand. For the first time, I would be the one to scribble a location on the back and hand these out. This, as much as anything else that had happened, felt like the entry to a new life.

A little after four, I met Eleanor back at Virginie's; I noticed that several more of the bunks were now draped with bags and possessions. "Do I have time to shower and change before we go?"

"Stacks of time," she replied. "Although if you want to wear anything elaborate for your show, you're welcome to leave it at my tent and change in the back. That's what Claire usually does."

"No fear of that." I had obviously not had the opportunity to plan any kind of costume, but at least I had a few things with me that seemed appropriate to face a crowd in; after my shower, I chose a simple black dress and knee-high boots. Looking in the mirror, I hoped that the audience wouldn't notice just how pale and jittery I was.

The route to the performance site was one I had not yet seen. "It's on a direct line between the dolmens," Eleanor explained, when I expressed surprise that we were heading away from the hill. "And aligned somehow with the Pierre Haina, and some other stones we didn't get to yesterday. There's a lot more of them scattered about."

The field, when we reached it, was partially screened off from the road by a windbreak of tall thin aspen trees, their quivering leaves just starting to turn from green to gold. But there was no disguising the fact that it was a hive of activity. The setup had to be quick, to preserve the mystery of how it was done, the illusion that it all sprung up out of the ground in the proverbial blink of an eye. Manon herself was standing at the back bumper of a large van, handing out parcels of cloth and string to an orderly queue of people. "Heather Ross," she called, spying me. "Join us here."

I fell in at the back of the line and took my turn to collect a bundle of silks. "Lay them out, on the ground, as you see others doing," she instructed. "And help expand them to size. Others will set them up."

It was all a very organized affair, and no one seemed to mind giving me instructions. Working in concert with more experienced magicians, I did my best to help transform the small rectangles of fabric into tents of virtually any size and shape required, and as fast as we did so, there was another group following along, raising them from the ground and adding supports where needed. By the time we had finished sizing the very last tent, I turned to see that nearly all of them had been coloured as well. "Can I do this last one?" I asked, turning back to see that it was already fully rigged up and ready.

The women I'd been working with – we'd been moving along so efficiently there had been no time for introductions – looked at each other. "Go ahead," one of them said, her accent difficult to place. "They'll all be adjusted later, once they're claimed."

I would need to be quick about it. But what colour? Closing my eyes and extending my hands, I pictured a favourite crayon shade from my childhood: the saturated pale purple of a Scottish thistle. I envisioned the hue drawing up through the ground, out my fingertips and spreading through the tent like a stain. When I opened my eyes again, I saw that it had worked, albeit slightly unevenly, leaving a rather tie-dyed effect.

"Lovely work." Coming up beside me, a man I hadn't seen before made a flicking hand gesture and a moment later the thistle-coloured tent was crowned with a spring-green pennant that suited it nicely. "You must be Heather. I'm Arthur Bradburn, Luke's dad." Now that he mentioned it, I could see the resemblance, though his hair was darker than his son's. "I hear you're collaborating."

I spread my hands out, palms up. "We're going to try."

The entire setup had been done in just under half an hour: about as close to instantaneously as anyone could hope for. A few people left straight away, and others were bustling back and forth between the field and the nearest house, presumably a staging ground of sorts, but most seemed to be taking a few minutes to admire our collective handiwork and to catch up with friends. I wandered up and down the newly-formed aisles for a little while, marvelling at what we had created, exchanging pleasantries with the few people I knew and a few others who introduced themselves. Part of my object in lingering, though, was to look for another familiar face: somehow I had been almost certain that this would be the day for Eric to turn up. However, he was nowhere in evidence. I had gotten this far without him, and I would have to trust that there would be other friendly faces around when the appointed hour came.

Luke and I had agreed to meet at seven-thirty to select a tent and set up; we would only attempt one performance that night, at around nine o'clock. Before any of that happened, I would need to prepare. First, I hastened across the village and up the trail to the Pierre Haina. Something about this spot, more than the other monuments around the area, spoke to me. This time I did put my hands on it, drawing the energy of the massive stone around myself like a cloak. From there, I took my time making my way back to the field. I could see the lights twinkling through the screen of trees, and headlights coming down the road, converging on the spot. Bypassing the ticket booth with a knowing nod, I heard whispers from the half-dozen people already queued up there. *Magicienne.*

No one had claimed the pale violet tent, and so we decided that it was as good a spot as any. We worked together to tweak it a bit, making it rounded instead of rectangular and adding a row of benches round the perimeter. Luke held out for two rows, but I thought that might be a bit optimistic for our first try at this - not to mention the fact that I was afraid that if I spent any more energy on accoutrements there would be nothing left for the performance.

He showed me a few tricks to light the tent up, though we wouldn't keep it lit till it was nearly time for our show, and we practised everything once more, to see if it would work as well within the tent as it had in the back of the barn at Gaetan's farm. It did.

"It's going to be great," he pronounced – though of course, he was hardly short on confidence. "Let's go see about some food."

My stomach was full of butterflies. "I don't know if I could eat right now."

Luke shook his head. "You should try, trust me. It's going to take a lot more power when there's a room full of people. It's best if you have at least a bite of something."

I let him persuade me, and we left the tent dark and set out to walk around the fair. As at Callanish, the Menagerie was one of the largest tents and took pride of place. Radiating out around it were pavilions of all shapes, sizes and colours – unrecognizable from what it had been only a few hours before. It was already almost full dark, and being dressed in black it was easy to slip around the crowds without attracting attention.

Luke pointed out a familiar orange tent – the Feast. Usually set up on the first and last days of a performance, it would contain a truly mind-boggling array of sweet and savoury delicacies. A line was already snaking out from the entrance, but he pointed around the back. "Not there. That stuff's tasty, but it won't do much for you, not when it's been stretched out so far. There's some actual non-magicked food for us."

Indeed, concealed at the back of the Feast tent there was a small side entrance that I doubted a stranger would be able to see. Stepping in, I relished the relative quiet for a moment, before selecting a toasted cheese sandwich and a large tumbler of punch from a completely prosaic-looking card table.

Claire popped out just after me, though I hadn't seen her go in. "That punch isn't alcoholic," she announced, sounding disappointed, after taking a sip from her own cup. "What time are you and Luke going on? Eleanor wants to try to pop by."

I looked around, but Luke seemed to have disappeared. "Around nine. You?"

"Not till later, so that's good – I can come see you as well. Good luck!"

I wished her the same, and made my way back towards our tent; I would save the other performances to watch I had gotten my own show done with.

Perhaps fifteen minutes before we intended to start, Luke illuminated the exterior of the tent, leaving the inside just barely light enough for people not to trip over the benches. There was a hidden vestibule at the back, almost a closet, where we could stash ourselves and await the moment to begin. Wanting to block out as many stimuli as possible, I closed my eyes and took deep, slow, regular breaths, in and out, as if I were meditating. I could still hear the shuffle of feet and the low murmur of voices, both inside and outside the tent, but I told myself they were nothing to do with me.

Eventually, he tapped me twice on the shoulder: our agreed-upon signal to begin. As we had practised, we first conjured up a low, resonant sound like the drone of a bagpipe. By holding my palms facing each other and squeezing the tension between them, I could modulate the tone up and down, creating a sort of background music. I maintained this as we emerged from the back into the centre of the tent, then let it abruptly drop. All eyes were upon us, the benches far fuller than I had anticipated, but I did not register anything beyond the presence of bodies, the anticipation in the air.

Luke raised his palms toward the apex of the tent, as did I. Drawing upon my own energy, the power from the ground beneath my feet, and the collective adrenaline of everyone in the room, I helped Luke produce a large sphere of swirling, multi-coloured light. As we threw our hands down between us, the ball was meant to shatter into its component parts, several dozen small orbs, each a different colour. It didn't resolve nearly as neatly as it had in practice, but I reminded myself that the audience didn't know what we had planned. After a few deep breaths, I managed to pull my rattled nerves together a bit, and get the swirling blobs of colour to look more rounded, even if they weren't as bright as I'd hoped. They bounced up and around us like a crashing wave; then, with carefully coordinated hand movements, we sent them moving around the tent, weaving in and out around the spectators – mostly successfully, although some crashed intangibly into people and disappeared. We brought the remaining spheres together and then apart, making them a little smaller and brighter with each repetition. Each pass worked a little better than the last, until the whole of the tent was swarming with tiny vivid dots like a horde of rainbow fireflies.

We were able to keep it going for what felt like a long time, but eventually my hands began to shake with the effort. Luke's face was tense. I gave him the briefest of nods; he matched it. Drawing our hands up one last time, we brought the tiny dots into a tight cloud. Casting our arms out and down, the dots skimmed along the floor towards the perimeter of the tent, then vanished, so that the space was briefly blacked out.

Luke brought the light back up, just to the level of a candle or two, and we stood back to back, then bowed deeply to the assembled company. As I stood back upright, a wave of applause broke over us. Able to register detail outside of myself for the first time in what seemed like hours, I noticed many familiar faces standing round the perimeter. Ben and Colleen were there, and Claire and Eleanor. There was Arthur, who I had met earlier, with a woman who I recognized as Luke's mother. They were still applauding; we bowed once more, to opposite sides of the tent this time, then made our exit.

We made off in opposite directions: a speedy departure from the vicinity of the tent before the audience could emerge. "They may see you around later," Luke had advised, "but if it seems like you vanish at the end of the performance, it keeps the mystery going. Besides, until you get way more used to this than either of us is, you'll be too knackered right after to deal with a bunch of people coming up and telling you what they think of your show. Split off and go lay low somewhere for half an hour or so."

I did just that, heading for a darkened tent on the very fringe of the field that served as a sort of backstage lounge, closed to the public. It looked mercifully empty; I kicked my boots off and stretched out at full length on a sofa. A glance at my watch told me that the seemingly never-ending performance had taken less than ten minutes. Exhausted, I closed my eyes. The moment I put my feet up on the armrest, though, I heard a disapproving noise. "What manners did they teach you, *trovatella*?"

I knew the voice, one that had directed that unidentified epithet at me once before. Isabella: the devoted daughter of my erstwhile great-grandfather Raffaele. What was she to me, then – a half-great-aunt? Just as I was debating whether to open my eyes or ignore her, a man's voice spoke up. "Leave the girl alone, Mama. Nonno said she's one of us." There was some further discussion in Italian, but their voices mercifully receded into the distance.

A few minutes later, as the adrenaline was starting to ebb away, replaced by a heaviness in my limbs that had me contemplating the wisdom of just going to sleep on the slightly-too-short couch, I heard a friendlier voice. "Nicely done, lady."

I opened my eyes and sat up, making room for Eleanor, but she was bustling around at the far end of the tent, and came over a minute later with a cup of tea for me. "That was a nice debut. Well executed, not too over the top. Congratulations. Here, have this; you look like you could use it."

The tea was milky and laced with sugar; I usually took it black, but right then it tasted just fine. "Did you have this many people looking out for you when you started?"

"Yes and no. New arrivals are so rare, you always wind up in a bit of a spotlight; the younger people want to glom onto you a bit and the older ones kind of reserve judgment. I didn't have Isabella slandering me in Italian, but then again, I didn't have the whole Kavanagh clan taking me under their collective wing, either, so I guess it evens out. As for me, I'm just delighted to have someone my own age – really my own age, not just looking like it and born who-knows-when – around here now. I've got to pop back and keep an eye on things, but I'm sure I'll see you around later. Drink your tea."

CHAPTER TEN

That first night, the rest of the show was a blur. I was gradually recovering from the exertion of performing, but it felt as if all my nerve endings had been rubbed with a fine sandpaper and left slightly raw. I retired to Virginie's – taking a bit of a wrong turn before I got my bearings – a little after midnight, while things were still in full swing. Falling asleep almost as soon as my head hit the pillow, I was haunted by strange dreams of masked faces and endless corridors.

The days after that fell into a pattern of sorts. Long walks around the village and up to the Pierre Haina in the mornings, sometimes with Eleanor or Claire, but often on my own. Afternoons practising with Luke, honing our act and adding little tweaks and modifications to it as my confidence grew. And evenings, of course, at the carnival. With the first night out of the way, I felt better able to bounce back after each performance, and spent part of my free time exploring the show, just as I had in Scotland. Some acts were the same, or only slightly varied; others were entirely novel. All were astounding and amazing, just as our cards promised. Behind the scenes, I did what I could to help pull my weight. Helping in the ticket booth was my favourite of the side jobs; it was a delight to watch the wonder and anticipation on the faces arriving.

Still, as enchanting as it all was, I felt Eric's absence like a missing limb, more and more with each passing night. He became the imaginary passenger on my journeys. Did he have ideas about the discordant energy around the dolmens, or the feeling of foreboding some people got when touching the smooth stone surface of the Devil's Bed? One morning at the Pierre Haina, a grey sky almost merging with the light mist that hovered over the fields, I found myself writing a note about the place on the back of one of the magician's cards; a miniature postcard, a snapshot of the moment. I tucked it into a pocket, separate from the others, no real purpose in mind.

When Ben met me in the street the following Tuesday – a week and a day after we had set up the show – and told me that it would be our last night in Wéris, I felt oddly relieved. Mostly because I had just about made it through my first outing as a fully-fledged magician, but partly because I felt that whatever our next stop was, perhaps it would bring Eric back.

Several people gathered in the hidden lounge tent for drinks on the last night, and I received a few congratulations on my successful entry into their world. I had just sat down with a fresh glass of wine when Luke draped himself onto a chair next to me. "Do you know where we're going next?"

"No. Do you?"

He frowned. "I was hoping you might. I've heard some rumours. Go on and ask Ben; he'll probably say."

"Go on and ask me what?" Ben came up behind us and sat down on Luke's other side.

"Apparently there are wild stories flying around, concerning our next destination," I explained.

Ben clapped Luke heavily on the shoulder. "All in good time, my boy. All in good time."

Luke snorted. "Nobody tells me anything."

"You're nineteen years old. What did you expect?" Laughing, Ben gave a nod in the direction of some of the other young people, who were playing cards at a table further away. "On you go, then."

After Luke went on his way, Ben pulled his chair closer. "I'm not surprised there are rumours. Something very... unusual... has come up."

"What is it?"

He shook his head. "Not here. In the morning, when I know more, we'll talk."

In the wee hours, we all joined forces to pack up the show. Shrinking the tents was somewhat harder than stretching them, but long before dawn the vans were packed and ready to be on their way to some unknown destination. The field was noticeably trodden down, but otherwise bore no sign of the spectacle it had played host to.

Ben had suggested that we regroup in the morning – after at least a couple of hours' sleep – for a walk, but it was clear as Claire and I caught up with her parents at the outskirts of the village that it was to be a meeting. Ben waited till we were making our way down a completely empty country lane before broaching the matters at hand. "We were supposed to have been going on to Denmark today or tomorrow, but plans have changed."

From the look on Colleen's face, she was as much in the dark as we were. "Well then, out with it."

"A message came." Ben stopped walking and looked at the three of us, his expression hard to read. "The Masquerade is going to be held again, for the first time in a half-century or more."

I looked to Claire for a clue, but she just shrugged. Even her mother looked none the wiser.

Getting no reaction, Ben sighed and continued. "I'd forgotten it was before your time, love. Now, I know you know," he began, looking at Colleen, before directing his attention to me and Claire. "But you may not, that we are not the only magicians out there."

"We're not?" As soon as I'd blurted it out, I realized how stupid it sounded, and resolved to hold my tongue.

"We're not. There's all manner of strange folk in the world. Some who keep themselves well outside of day-to-day life, and others who for all the world seem to be perfectly normal. We don't often cross paths. At least so far as we know – after all, we make ourselves out to be quite normal a good bit of the time as well. But the thing is, every now and then – once in a great while – we're all of us invited to Venice, to a masquerade ball."

Claire and I exchanged looks. "Why?" she asked.

It was Ben's turn to shrug. "Why do anything? I don't know who hosts it, or what their aim is. See and be seen, maybe. Show off. There's only been one before in my lifetime, when I was a younger man. It's the night of nights, I can tell you."

"And are we all invited?" Claire asked, looking back and forth between her parents.

"Yes, but…" He took a deep breath. "I've talked with the others, and we've agreed: only those who have taken the Magician's Walk should go."

"That's not you, my girl," Colleen said, looking slightly relieved.

Colour rose to Claire's cheeks. "I'll do it right now."

"I don't think you're ready, Claire."

"I'm twenty-six years old, Mother…"

71

At that, Ben touched my arm. "Walk this way," he said, inclining his head away from his wife and daughter. "Let's leave them to it."

"So, what's this Magician's Walk?" I asked, when we had gone a little way down the road. "I'm guessing you think I should do it – and probably that Claire should, too – or you wouldn't have brought us out here for this conversation."

"True," he said. "Claire'll wear her mum down in good time, and save me the trouble. As for yourself: aye, I think you should, but only you can say if you're ready or not. As for what it is... Have you ever heard of something called a vision quest?"

"I studied anthropology. Of course I have." Belatedly, I remembered Manon's words about taking a journey of discovery. Was that what this was to be?

"It's something we do, usually some time in your first few years as a magician – and then sometimes again, for those who feel they need to. Claire really should have done, by now, but she was away for a few years – and, well, you know how mums are. Colleen doesn't always want to admit that her baby is a grown woman. But I'm sure she will now – and most of the other young folk – what with the Masquerade coming. They'll all want to go, no doubt."

I had any number of questions about this masquerade ball, but left them aside for the moment. "So, this... walk, this vision quest thing. I'm sure the end result is different for different people, so I'm not asking about that, but what exactly is involved?" I knew that vision quests took all sorts of forms in different cultures: fasting, exposure to the elements, sensory deprivation, physical exertion, sometimes hallucinogens. Not for the first time, I wondered if I really had any idea what I'd gotten myself into.

"You have to have an elder with you," he began. "Someone experienced, or you'll never find the place you need to begin. You fast for the day leading up to it. At sunset, you walk out into the

72

forest, and you walk there through the night. Who or what comes to walk with you… that's different for everyone."

"That's it?" It came out sounding more flippant than I'd intended.

He cocked his head. "It's not so simple, when it comes to it. You come through the night a wiser person, one way or the other, but sometimes someone's not prepared for what they find. Sometimes they don't make it through the night, and have to call for their companion to come and get them."

"And what if that happens?"

"Just means they weren't ready. There's no shame in it; they just go back and train some more, and try again when the time is right. Like not making your driver's exam the first go. That's usually kids, though. The nineteen- or twenty-year-olds who think they've got the world figured out. I don't think that'll be you."

I certainly didn't think I had the world figured out, in any case. "So I would walk out into the forest. Is this something that can be done any time, in any forest?"

Ben shook his head. "Almost any time. The day or two around a full moon, though it's best if the weather's dry, for all concerned. But not just any forest. The Black Forest."

With everything else going on, the last thing I'd thought to pay attention to was the moon. "When is the next full moon?"

"Saturday night. October the nineteenth."

Three days away. The rest of my training so far had been accelerated; I might as well jump straight into this as well. "And when is this… Masquerade?"

He laughed. "The thirty-first, darling. When else?"

CHAPTER ELEVEN

There was not much to do to prepare for the Magician's Walk, as far as anyone could tell me. There was no point in travelling back to Ireland, only to have to turn right around and head to Germany, but we took a ride with Eleanor as far as Brussels, where we stayed the night in a cheap hotel and picked Molly and Daniel up at the station first thing the next morning. On hearing of the Magician's Walk, they had immediately offered to come to Germany and act as elders for Claire and myself. "It's a big forest," Daniel explained. "You'll all start somewhere a wee bit different. Like life."

That was all he would say on the matter, but the Masquerade was almost the only topic of discussion as we crowded into a rented minivan and began the drive back south towards Germany. "Oh, we'll go, of course," Molly said, when it first came up. "We've had a letter as well."

She retrieved it from her purse and showed it to me: heavy, old-fashioned vellum, with a wax seal and elegant calligraphy, addressed to *Daniel and Molly Kavanagh* but without any location details of any kind. "How did this get to you?" I asked, dismissing Hollywood visions of owls.

"Same as it ever has," Daniel replied. "On the doorstep. Doesn't really matter where in the world you are: if you're magical, you'll have an invite. If we'd been with the troupe, we'd have been included in that letter, same as all of you."

Beside me in the back row of the van, Claire gave me a look and silently mouthed *Eric?* I had been thinking the same thing, but really had no idea. Raising my eyebrows, I gave a fractional shrug.

"Anywhere in the world," Daniel repeated, though I wasn't sure if he had seen us or not.

After a while we all lapsed into silence, but another question buzzed around in the back of my mind until I finally had to ask it. "Ben, can I ask you something? It's not about the Magician's Walk."

"Of course," he replied.

"Not to be rude, but... Okay, you said yourself that you're nearly ninety, and you look like you're in your early sixties at the absolute most."

"Thank you, darling." He and his father both laughed.

"Yes, well. But... you had to show identification to rent the car, right? And things like driver's licenses and passports and stuff. Isn't there a certain point where your birthdate and your appearance can't be explained away by lucky genes and taking good care of yourself?"

"Yeah, Dad," Claire added, in a tone that suggested she had asked this before, and not been given an answer. "How do you do that, exactly?"

"We have a friend in London," Ben replied, "who takes care of those sorts of things for us. But you don't need to worry about anything like that just yet. Although Heather, if you need some help for a work permit or what-have-you, we can talk."

"I think I'm okay for now, thanks." At some point I would have to find a place in the UK, where I could claim residency, get a bank account, and all sorts of other mundane things that I didn't really want to think about just yet. Instead, I sat back and looked out the window as a modest sign announced our crossing from Belgium into Luxembourg.

From Luxembourg we passed through a corner of France, till eventually we hit the German border just past Strasbourg. Shortly after that, we were in the Black Forest region. It was not the endless dark woods I might have pictured, but a pretty landscape of steep forested hills flanking manicured valleys. In one of these valleys, we came to a halt in a settlement about the size of Wéris, and checked into a small inn. The remainder of that day, and the next, we acted as though we were on holiday, exploring hiking trails near the village and enjoying the food and the views. On Saturday morning, though, Colleen woke Claire and me before dawn.

"Have a little bite of toast and tea now," she suggested. "Once the sun rises, you'll fast for the day, though you can have water whenever you like. Then just rest up, or even take a nap if you feel you can. It'll be a long night."

Claire was happy to go straight back to sleep, but I was restless; I paced the room for a while before getting dressed and heading outside. The village was quiet, the hour still early, the light quite different from that of Wéris. Not knowing how much physical exertion the Magician's Walk might demand, I didn't want to do anything too taxing, but walking helped settle my wound-up nerves. A path led out of the village, up a grassy slope to the very edge of the forest; I followed that. Around a bend, just before the trail led into the trees, there was a bench, with a familiar figure slouched on it. I sat down next to him. "Alright, Luke?"

He took a deep breath, sitting up a bit straighter, but picking nervously at his nails. "Yeah. This is just a formality, right?"

"I'm thinking it'll probably be some kind of learning experience. Otherwise why would we do it? All the same, I'll be glad to have it over with."

He nodded. "Me too."

We sat there for most of the morning – sometimes chatting about inconsequential things, but mostly just sitting, watching the movement of the light and cloud over the village below. When he took his leave of me, I stayed a little longer, pulling a pen and a magician's card from my pocket and summing up in tiny writing my few lingering fears about the step I was about to take.

I wasn't used to fasting, though; eventually I did start to feel a little light-headed, and decided it would be wise to head back to the hotel until it was time to go. Surprisingly, I slept. When I woke again the afternoon was well advanced and my head felt clearer. No one had told me it needed to be done, but I took a long shower, feeling that it was important to be clean to start this journey, and opted for something comfortable and warm to wear. According to the weather report, the sun would set at around six-thirty. At five-forty-five, Daniel knocked on the door. "Time to go. Best bring your coats."

Ben drove us up the hill, into the forest, letting Claire and Molly off at a seemingly random point along the road. "Good luck, sweetheart. Will you be warm enough, Mum?"

Molly made a 'tsk' noise. "I'm not so frail that I can't spend a night out of doors, now. I've got my thermos flask and my wool jumper. Away with you."

Perhaps two or three kilometres down the road, he pulled off again. "Do I need luck?" I asked, before he could say it.

"No, but humour me. I need something to say," Ben replied, chuckling. "See you on the other side, then."

We were high up in the hills, and with evergreens stretching toward the sky in every direction there was no panorama, only glimpses of the darkening sky above. Daniel walked with me a little way in from the road, till we saw around us only trees. "Don't be afraid, my dear," he said, his voice hushed. "No matter what you see. There are no dangers in the forest: only what you bring with you, and to you. If you feel you need to stop the walk before sunrise, you need only call out my name and I will be there, straight away. But I don't think you'll need me, once the way is opened."

He put his aged hand to my cheek for a moment, then turned his back, raising his hands to the sky. There were some words, low, that I could not understand, and then he walked around the tiny clearing we stood in, touching the bark of each tree as he passed. I looked around, waiting for some sign, some indication of what to do next.

After a few moments, a faint glow lit the ground between two straight old trunks. I looked around for Daniel, but he seemed to have gone. The light did not get brighter, but it slowly spread along the ground, forming something like a pathway. This, then, must be the Magician's Walk. Holding myself very still, I took several slow, deep breaths, then a step forward.

The pale glow was just visible enough – barely - to follow. I walked on for what seemed like a very long time without anything happening, though I was reaching out with all my senses for anything out of the ordinary. Was this it? If I simply walked on and on, all night, with nothing happening, would I have succeeded or failed? I lost all sense of time, almost all sense of myself. At times I wondered if I was dreaming this walk, or perhaps dreaming everything that had happened – the journey, the magicians, all of it. Perhaps there had never been anything else but this, this darkness, the endless nighttime trees.

When I first saw the man, I assumed him to be part of the dream.

But then I shook myself, remembering the capacity for conscious thought. *Don't be afraid*, I had been told. Was this part of the path?

As I walked closer, he turned around to face me. The man was tall, dark-haired – brown or black hair, I could not tell in the dim – and there was something about him that bore just a whisper of familiarity. Fifteen feet away, I stopped. Near enough to speak, far enough for safety; I regarded him, wondering what had led him across my path.

He squinted at me, and stepped two paces forward. Scowling slightly, he spoke. "Do I know you, lass?"

I did not know his voice, but the accent was broad Glasgow, unmistakable. And then I realized who he reminded me of: my dad as a young man. *There is only what you bring with you, or to you.* "You're Don Ross," I said, only knowing it with certainty as the words came out of my mouth. If he had not died young, he would be ninety-two. This man looked to be in his thirties. Don Ross as he had died, then. "Are you a ghost?"

"Are you?" There was a trace of defiance, of challenge, in his voice, as he took another step forward and studied me as I was studying him. "Since you know my name, then give me yours, hen."

I straightened up to my full height. Not as tall as he, but tall for a woman: I had this height from my dad, who had it from him. He had it from Raffaele. We were linked, all of us. "Heather Ross. I was born in nineteen-seventy-five. Your son Andrew is my father."

The fight went out of him entirely, instantly. "Is that so, then? Is that so?" His voice was softer. "And then why would you be after sending for me?"

As far as I knew, I had done nothing of the sort, but found myself reluctant to say so. There must be a reason why Don Ross – his spirit? his ghost? – was here, in the Schwarzwald, in the middle of the night, talking to me. "There are things I want to ask you." That much was true. I motioned to a fallen log amongst the trees. "Maybe we should sit. Can you sit?"

Don laughed, and in that moment his face became friendly. "Like Marley's ghost, aye? Aye, I can sit."

We sat down on the log and I thought for a while about what it was that I wanted to know. Everything, really. But I didn't know how long we had, or what he might answer. "Do you know who your father was?"

He was silent for a long while, the scowl back on his face. But he replied. "In my day that was an impertinent question to ask a man. Fights've been started over less. You get asked that question a lot, when you're a boy wi' no dad. When I was a wean, my mum said my dad had been a fisherman out of Stornoway pier, drowned when his boat went down before I was born. That's what she told them all. Said he was Don Ross, and me named for him. But I found out later, that was the story of her dad, not mine. But she had to say something, didn't she?"

"Of course."

"Then one day she ran across somebody she knew, somebody who knew her from Lewis and put the lie to her story, knew that she was plain Ina Ross, never married. And somehow everyone knew it. By the time I went to school, they all knew." He shook his head. "Mum used to do fancy work – sewing, like – for some ladies, but that all seemed to dry up once they knew she was a fallen woman and not a respectable young widow. Then she took in washing. Sometimes when that wasn't enough to keep us fed, well..." Don looked away, not finishing that thought. "I got in a lot of fights, near every day. I didn't care so much what they said about me, but when they started in about my mum... Black Don, they called me, and not just for my hair, you ken. Thing was," he continued, "when I got angry, things would happen. I lost my temper in our room one day and a glass bottle broke, on the ledge, nowhere near where I was. Mum damn near lost her mind. Whacked me about the head with her hairbrush, saying 'you're like him, you're just like him'. Screaming and crying, like. So when she stops, I ask her: who was my dad? Who?"

"And did she answer?"

"She cried and cried, and she said he was the devil. Well, I was eleven years old and I wasn't sure I quite believed that, and I said so. Then she said he was an evil man, and had powers that could only've come from the devil. Made me promise to never do that again, said she didnae want me to go to the devil like the man who fathered me."

"Was that all she said?"

"Aye, well… After that, if she got mad enough – especially when she was in her cups, mind – she'd sometimes threaten me, that if I didn't smarten up, didn't stop getting in fights and stealing sweets and breaking windows, that she'd find the devil man and leave me with him. Let him make shift to look after me. And I never wanted that. She was a hard woman, you ken. She had a hard lot in life. But we loved each other in our way, Mum and me. I wanted to get a job and look after her, let her rest for once in her life, but there wasn't a job to be had, not till the war started. I was eighteen and they'd give me food and board and a wage, so I signed up. Sent most of my pay to my mum."

"And you were discharged."

He narrowed his eyes. "You know some things about me. You've done some digging, or someone has. Aye, I was discharged. Did they tell you why?"

I shook my head.

"I did alright in the navy. Made it till 'forty-four, almost the end. And then I got word my mum was gone. Hit by a lorry, they said, in the street. And everything I'd been holding in – all through the war, all through the years they called me bastard, all the times she said she'd leave me with the devil man – I couldn't hold it in any more. They said I'd cracked. Sent me home. But where was I going to go? I knocked around Glasgow till I could get passage to Canada, after the war was done. Thought I could start all over in a new place, where nobody knew about my mum or the devil man or Black Don Ross. And you know, I thought it was going to work. I met wee Jean MacDonald, and we married. Her mum never quite took to me, but her dad, he got me a job on the line at Goodrich. We had three kids, a house… it should have been the perfect life. Except for me. I was still cracked, you see."

Brushing a hand across his eyes, he shook his head. "I loved Jeannie. I did. And I was so damned proud of my son, and my two wee daughters, and it'd be like I was thinking all the right things inside and doing all the wrong things outside. I still remember seeing the grille of that car coming at me, that night. I was coming off shift and it was sleeting; I don't even know if they saw me till they hit me. And when I was laying there, I felt it all leaving me. The anger. There were times when anger kept me alive, but it mostly just kept me from living. And I thought if I could just do it again, I could be a good man. But we don't all get a second chance."

I wanted to say that perhaps this was a second chance, of a sort, but found that my voice wouldn't quite come.

"Jeannie… she'd be your gran, I guess," he said, after a while. "I don't even know what year this is. Is she living still?"

"Yes. It's twenty-thirteen. She's eighty-nine now, and still very much a going concern."

He nodded. "Did she ever marry again?"

I wasn't sure what answer he wanted to hear. "She did. He's still living too, a man named Marcel, from Montreal. They got married when my dad was still young."

"And is he a good man, this Marcel? Was he good to the kids?"

"Yes. And to the grandkids. I have a younger sister; Aunt Nancy has three boys and Aunt Janet has a boy and a girl."

"Is that so?" He shook his head. "I'm glad Jeannie found a good man for her, and for the kids. I was never able to be that man."

I wondered what kind of man he might have been if Ina really had made good on her threats, and left him with the magicians, in Raffaele's care. He almost certainly had had magical talents that could have been channeled into beauty, instead of erupting in rage, leaving him doubting his own sanity. Of course, if that had happened, I would not exist. Part of me wanted to explain it all to him, to tell him about Raffaele, the magicians, everything. "I think you could have been a different man," I said at last. With some trepidation, I reached out and took his hand and was a little surprised to find it solid. "Under different circumstances."

He smiled again, and suddenly I saw him as an old man – the man he might have been if he had gotten that second chance, if he had survived and grown old with his family and been known to me as a grandfather – and then a moment later, the illusion was gone. I was sitting alone on a log in the forest, but for just a moment, I still heard his voice. "Aye, lass. Maybe you're right."

CHAPTER TWELVE

I sat on the log in the dark, shaken by my encounter with my long-lost grandfather. There had been more to his story, clearly, things he'd been unwilling to say – but even the brief account he'd given had hit me like a brick to the head. Intellectually, I had known that Ina Ross must have had a hard life, but it was quite different to have it spelled out for me by an eyewitness. And with what he had had to go on, no wonder Don had thought himself 'cracked'.

And still, I wondered why the Magician's Walk had brought us together. Was it for my benefit, or his?

All idea of time had long since eluded me, but it was still dark. The shade of Don Ross showed no inclination to return, and the faintly illuminated path still lay before me. I stood up and walked on. This forest had a scent, of evergreen and moss and damp undergrowth to be sure, but something else as well, something I couldn't place. I walked on, my feet silent beneath me, pondering my grandfather's story and trying to put my finger on exactly what the elusive smell was. It grew stronger as I continued along the path, as if I were coming closer to its source. And then I realized where I knew it from. I walked faster, finding new energy. And around a bend in the path, there she was.

There was no hesitation this time. "Granny Chrissie!"

She was recognizably my great-grandmother, but not as frail as she had been when I saw her last. This was the way I remembered her from my childhood, down to the tea-rose perfume. "Heather! You found them, then?"

"Yes." There was no question in my mind who 'they' were. We embraced, my tall frame dwarfing her tiny one, as always. It had been so long. "It took a long time, but they came back. I found them."

Her eyes searching my face, she nodded. "I knew you would. I always knew it would be you."

There was something I had to ask her, I realized. "Did you know about Don Ross? Did you know that he was...?"

"He was Ina's child after all, wasn't he?" she said, her voice low. "And Raffaele's. I had always wondered, but I didn't want to believe it. Poor girl."

"I met him. I mean... I met Don, just now, here, but not that. I met Raffaele. I was there when he died. Before... before he passed, he told me everything." I watched her expression, wondering if she knew the whole story. Had she ever suspected her own parentage? I thought not. "He knew he was wrong, in how he treated you. Both of you."

Granny Chrissie waved it away. "That's as may be. It was water under the bridge for me in any case, and long since too late for Ina. But if I know the magicians live on with you: that'll suit me fine, lass. Will you show me a trick?"

To almost anyone else, I might have protested that I knew too little, that I was still just learning. "It's not much," I warned, then tried one of the illusions that Luke and I had used in our performance. On my own, it was much smaller, just a spray of coloured sparkles that faded away in a few seconds, but by their light my great-grandmother was transformed. She didn't change her appearance, as Don had, but I could see the young girl that had lived on within her.

"Oh, well done!" she said, applauding. "I knew it. I always did, Heather. Now, I haven't much time…"

She seemed to be fading, growing insubstantial before my eyes. But I had stayed such a long time with Don – it didn't seem fair. "No! Granny Chrissie, stay, please."

Shaking her head, she smiled. "I'm past my time. There's someone else to see you, someone who needs to speak with you more. This isn't the end of your journey, you know; it's only the beginning. You just carry on, Heather. That's a good girl."

And, once again, I was alone in the forest. There was nothing for it but to walk on.

For a third time, I was forging ahead through the woods until it began to feel like sleepwalking. But this time I knew that there was someone ahead. I couldn't think who it could be. Don Ross had been a shock, to be sure, but in retrospect he had been a loose end in my family story, so perhaps it made sense. Granny Chrissie – if anyone was going to come and walk this path with me, of course it had been her. But who else? I had met Raffaele, and he had done his best to clear his account with me before his passing; I did not expect to encounter him. But Sébastien? Perhaps he was the one. If it was him, could he still use his magic, decades after his death? I'd been told that he could influence people, affect what they were thinking: a sort of mind trick. Should I be wary? I wasn't sure.

When I finally saw a person up ahead, my first thought was that he was too tall to be Sébastien – which was absurd, because I did not know anything about Sébastien's appearance. I supposed I was making an assumption because his illegitimate daughter, my

Granny Chrissie, had been so slight in stature. But he also looked far too modern, I realized on a second glance. This was not a man who had died in the nineteen-thirties, but perhaps one who had been born then. He had close-cropped grey hair, a strong jaw and a nose that looked like it had been broken at least once. Despite his age and his casual clothing, his posture was ramrod-straight, as though he were standing at attention. His left hand, I realized, was missing the pinky finger. I walked up to within six feet of him, and there was still absolutely nothing about him that was familiar.

"Hello," I said.

When he smiled, I felt more comfortable. "Hello. I was wondering when I would run into someone out here. Are you… Heather?"

The accent came from my side of the Atlantic. How did this man know who I was? "Yes."

He held out his hand. "I'm John. John Heyward."

Midway through shaking his hand, I froze. "Eric's father? But… does that mean you're…?"

He nodded. "Afraid so. Last week. Had a heart attack a month ago, and the docs thought I was recovering, but I guess the old ticker had just had enough."

I swallowed hard. "I'm sorry."

"Well, I had a good run. What can you do? Now, you're one of these magicians, aren't you?"

"Yes… wait. How did you know that?"

John smiled. "Well, Eric and I had some long talks, there in the hospital. He told me everything – or at least, the parts that matter. I'd always wondered if that might be what really kept him in Europe all these years. Now I understand."

I didn't know if I did. "Then... why are you here? Why me? Why not Claire?" If he was going to appear to anyone doing the Magician's Walk on this particular night, surely she had a stronger connection to his son.

"Claire... that's his other little sister." John nodded. "He told me about her, and about his... other father. He's spent almost half his life with them now. Do you know this Ben Kavanagh? I'm sure he must have been charming, if Anne loved him all those years ago. But is he a good man?"

"Yes," I replied, without hesitation. "And... well, I admit I've only known them a little while, but I don't think Ben has ever tried to take your place. He said to me that you're the only one who gets to claim the title of dad."

John sighed, and leaned up against the trunk of a tree, and something about his movement was uncanny: Eric might have Ben's DNA, but he had taken a lot from this man as well. "From the day I asked Anne to marry me, I swore that I'd never treat that child as anything other than my own, and I can honestly say that I'm pretty sure I lived up to that. She worried that things would change, once we had Trevor and Dawn, but for me, it never did. Truth be told, Eric was a hard act for the other kids to live up to, even though I don't think he ever knew it. Guess I know now that it must have had something to do with having magic in his blood." He went silent for a few seconds. "It was weighing on him so heavily, when he came home. He felt so guilty about having been away all these years. I tried to set him straight, tell him he was doing what he was always meant to do, but I know he'll take it hard. He's hard on himself."

I thought of what Manon had said to me. "It's a good quality, for a magician."

"Well, I suppose that makes sense. It was a good quality in the Air Force, too, so who knows, maybe that's something I can say he got from me. Listen, Heather," he added, glancing over his shoulder. "It'll be daylight sooner than you think, so I haven't got a lot of time. Look out for my son, will you? He's going to need a friend, when he gets back."

"Are you sure he's coming back?" I asked, voicing that fear out loud for the first time.

John looked at me and laughed softly. "I'm sure. He might have to take some time to get things in order, and make sure that Anne's alright, but he'll be back."

He shook my hand once more, this time enclosing my one hand in both of his, then turned and strode away, pausing once to wave just before he disappeared round a bend.

The path was not glowing so brightly any longer; I was able to follow it a little further before I realized that I was simply seeing trodden-down earth under my feet. It was slightly less dark, the glimpses of sky overhead blue now instead of black. Somewhere off in the distance, a bird began to sing.

My way took me through the dense woods a while longer, but finally the trees thinned and I came out to a clearing at the forest's edge, blinking at the first rays of the rising sun.

"Well done, my dear." Daniel was waiting there, half-hidden in the rapidly-disappearing shadows. "You've come through the night."

I had successfully completed the Magician's Walk. So had Claire, and Luke. The mood was decidedly celebratory around the three of us as we returned to the village and gathered for a large breakfast in the hotel's otherwise-empty dining room, but I could see that both of them were still deep in thought over whatever it was that they had experienced. The tradition, I had been told, was not to ask anyone about their night in the woods; I wondered if it was similarly taboo to volunteer the information.

The truth was, though I had been profoundly affected by the three meetings, I was still puzzling over the meaning of the whole thing. I wasn't sure what I had really expected: some kind of universal truth about what it meant to be a magician, or what the source of our power was, perhaps. Instead, I had learned a bit more about my grandfather's life, had a brief reunion with Granny Chrissie, and come face-to-face with the sad news that Eric's father had indeed passed away. I had gained some knowledge, certainly, but I wasn't sure why. I hadn't even thought to ask any of the three of them about death, or the afterlife, or anything of the sort.

Looking down into my cup of tea, I ran over the conversations in my mind, trying to pull out a common thread. They had had as many questions for me as I'd for them. Don Ross had seemed as though he had been waiting a long time to tell his side of the story, and to know what had become of his family. *Is she living still? Did she marry again? Was he good to the kids?* For Granny Chrissie, it had been confirmation that she sought – I had found the magicians at last; I was one myself. The mission she had set me on her deathbed had been fulfilled.

And John Heyward. He had had questions, too: about the other half of his son's double life, whether he was among good people who cared for him. Whether someone would look out for him as he recovered from the loss of his father. Whatever John had gleaned from our short meeting, it seemed that he'd trusted me; he had left happier, reassured.

So had Granny Chrissie, and Don Ross, now that I thought about it. Whatever else the Magician's Walk had been about, at least I had been able to give that gift to the three of them.

And then I sat up straight, so abruptly that I jostled the breakfast table and nearly upset a few cups. "Are you alright, love?" Molly asked.

"Yes... sorry. Yes, I'm fine," I replied. "I've just... realized something."

That was it. Through the strange, meditative night, I had made three people happy. What had happened on anyone else's vision quest was a mystery, but for me, this was the message of the Magician's Walk, suddenly as clear as day. *It wasn't about me.* It was about what my gift could do for other people, even if that was as simple as giving a performance that could take someone's mind off their troubles for a moment. It didn't matter who my ancestors were, or what I might be running away from in my own former life, or whether or not a few other magicians wanted me there. It was about facing outwards instead of in – maybe for the first time.

We returned to Fernwood, and for the first few days I had the sense that everyone was handling Claire and me with the proverbial kid gloves as we processed our separate experiences in the Black Forest. I told no one about what I had seen, but I did sit down with pen and paper and write a long letter to my dad. In it, I tried to impart a little of what I had learned about Don Ross – implying that I had come across this information through some research along my travels. I supposed that speaking directly with the dead was a form of 'research', after all. And talking to John had reminded me that I still had a role to play in my family back home, even if I was going to have to figure out a new way to do that.

I still didn't have any details to offer about when I would be home next. Though I vaguely had it in mind to go back to Canada for Christmas, and to apply for my UK residency then, I was loath to make any firm plan until after Eric returned; John Heyward had laid that responsibility on my shoulders and I did not intend to let him down. *I'm staying with some friends in Ireland,* I wrote, *at a beautiful old house in the country, south of Dublin. We're going to take a little trip down to Venice for Halloween.* Considering this, I had second thoughts: was

I saying too much? Picking up my half-finished letter, I found Ben in the library and asked for his thoughts on the matter.

"Oh, no, that's fine," he said. "There's all sorts of reasons to go to Venice, and it's not like your dad's going to have any idea that the Masquerade is going on. You might not always want to go into the whole itinerary every time we travel, or somebody might start to put two and two together – but then again, they might not. And really, only you know how much to say, or not say; I don't know your dad. You'll have to decide for yourself how much to tell your family about exactly what we do, but you can't shut them out completely. I mean, I've never asked, myself, but Eric's mum must have at least some idea of what he's up to, seeing as how he came into the world, and how she almost came to join us once. At any rate," he added, "you can certainly feel free to give this as your address, for as long as you like, and let your people get in touch with you here, if they prefer the post rather than the computer. In case you haven't noticed, we've made you an honorary Kavanagh, whether you like it or not."

Chuckling, he went back to the book he had spread open on the table. I only belatedly noticed what it was – a volume of sketches of elaborate costumes and masks, its pages yellowed and ragged round the edges. "These are for the Masquerade, aren't they?"

He nodded. "Ideas, at any rate. Mum had something like this, she told me, once back before I was born." Pointing at a deep green ball gown, he studied the page a moment longer before flipping to the next. "All the Venetian masquerades – whether magic or no – have a tradition, when it comes to the costumes. But the mask is the thing."

"Where will we get clothes like this?" I asked. I imagined that something so beautiful would be kept, and perhaps one day worn again, but I certainly would not fit into the hand-me-downs of anyone in the household.

"It's a costume house. In Venice," he said. "Some of the family were travelling magicians, once, but they found their talents were well suited for costume, and that they could make a far better living staying put. They remember their roots, though. When the Masquerade comes round, we just need to pay them a visit and they'll fit us out for the night."

I took a moment to finish my letter to my father, and got it ready to put in the mail, then came back to look through the book of costumes. Claire joined me after a while, and Ben left us to it. The illustrations were gorgeous, but it was hard, if not impossible, to picture myself in any of them.

"Do you think everyone will really be wearing Marie Antoinette ballgowns to the floor?" I asked.

"Not the men, I expect," Claire joked. "Honestly, I don't know. This book has got to be a hundred years old, so maybe they've modernized a bit? But given that we're just borrowing things for one evening, I guess we can't be too fussy."

I flipped past another page of dresses. "Even my wedding dress wasn't half this fancy," I mused.

"You're married?" she exclaimed.

"Was. I'm divorced." I was surprised that I hadn't mentioned it to her before; then again, it felt like ancient history to me at times already. "Less said about him the better. What do you think we actually do at this masquerade? These dresses are beautiful, but I can't imagine doing much in them but standing around. Certainly not doing any magic."

"We'll probably mostly be watching, I think." She ran her finger over a picture of an elaborate golden gown, then shook her head and turned the page. "We'll be a bit out of our league, from what I've heard. Look at that one: how would you even get through the door with a skirt that wide?"

We perused in silence for a while, before she spoke again, in quite a different tone. "I almost got married. When I was living in Dublin, after uni. That was why I stayed away so long. He was lovely, but I finally realized that I couldn't face being a normal person forever."

I didn't want to pry. "You're right. Being normal is quite overrated."

CHAPTER THIRTEEN

Standing in the middle of the room, I looked at the garments laid out before me. The thirty-first of October had come, and I was in a bedroom on the third floor of a Venetian house, with a view over red-tiled rooftops towards the spire of a small church. Claire, Eleanor and I were sharing a small apartment in the attic of the building, while Ben, Colleen, Molly and Daniel were staying downstairs in the main part of the house with the owner, another of these hospitable friends that they seemed to have everywhere.

The Masquerade would start at sunset, but apparently it was customary to take our time getting there, taking the opportunity to walk the streets clad in costume and mask despite the fact that this was well outside the traditional Carnival season. Hence, we had all retired to our rooms to wrangle with the unfamiliar clothing.

Our visit to the costume house had been surprisingly businesslike; a young woman had taken my measurements, yelled something in Italian to someone in another room, and a few minutes later I'd been given a choice of four outfits. I had rejected three Cinderella gowns in favour of a vaguely medieval ensemble that thankfully did not have a skirt wider than my arm span. At the sound of a tap at the door, I hastily slipped the long black chemise – thin and loose like a nightgown – over my head. "Come in."

It was Eleanor, staying true to her usual style in a dress that could have come from a nineteen-forties Hollywood red carpet. "Can you zip me up?"

I obliged, and got her to help me lace myself into the violet overdress: not quite a corset, but it was snug all the same. "Do you feel as weird as I do about everyone wearing masks?"

She gave me a strange look. "It's quite glamorous, really."

Picking up my half-mask, purple to match the outfit, I ran my finger over its intricate edges. "At least we can talk, and eat, in these. The other ones freak me out a little." The classic Venetian mask covered the whole face, creating an eerily blank look. "Can you help me do something with my hair?"

An hour later, there was a knock on the door: time to go. It was still warm in the late afternoon sunshine, particularly in my heavy dress; I hoped it would cool off as the evening advanced. We were a striking group, I had to admit. Looking around, I tried to memorize what everyone was wearing, so that I would still recognize them in the crowd later. Molly in dove-grey and Colleen in peacock blue; Claire in a shimmering dark green; Ben and his father in old-fashioned knee breeches, velvet frock coats, and three-cornered hats, Daniel with a grey cloak over top. Both of the older women wore full face masks, decorated to match their outfits, but Ben wore a strange mask that slanted outwards from the cheekbones down, and Daniel's had a long protruding beak like a medieval plague doctor. I was relieved when he took it off for a moment to kiss Claire on the cheek.

"You look beautiful, darling. And Eleanor, you're a vision, as always. You too, Heather."

Daniel replaced his mask as the water taxi pulled up, and extended his hand to help all the women step down into the boat. Passersby stopped to look as the small open craft full of costumed magicians slipped past, down the waterway and out into the Grand Canal. We turned left, down a much smaller canal, spanned occasionally by arched pedestrian bridges, and pulled up at a jetty near some traditional gondolas. "Walk on, and don't say a word," Ben whispered from behind his mask, before paying the boatman.

A number of tourists were waiting to board the gondolas, and several of them began to snap our pictures; one young man popped out in front of me and Claire and tried to take a selfie, but out of the corner of my eye I saw Eleanor make a subtle gesture. I suspected his photo would not turn out. As we followed Ben down the narrow alleyways of the old city, I began to see other costumed individuals here and there, their outfits too elaborate to give away any hint of who might be beneath. Finally, we came to an open plaza fronting onto yet another waterway. Here, a large group of masked magicians waited, as a nearly-continuous line of gondolas took their turns collecting passengers. These were not the typical sightseeing vessels, though; each was manned by a boatman in full masquerade regalia, who piloted the craft by hand movements alone.

The seven of us were too many to go together, so Eleanor and I got into the next boat, behind the Kavanaghs. We were joined by a man and woman who looked about our own age, at least from what I could tell behind their half-masks. To my great surprise, they had a little girl with them, who couldn't be more than seven or eight. She was masked as well, and wore a pale blue crown that matched her taffeta party dress. The parents – for clearly, they were a family – patted a seat for her to sit between them. Sitting down, the girl whispered something in her father's ear, at which he uncurled his fingers to reveal a tiny flame in the palm of his hand. Her mother gave a small shake of the head, with an expression of *not right now* that was readable even from behind a mask, though she was smiling as well.

The gondola came up alongside a long, unremarkable grey building that looked like some kind of an old warehouse; it had an archway opening directly onto the water and the boatman silently navigated the turn to take us through it to a private jetty. Ahead we could see the Kavanaghs disembarking and waiting for us to catch up. We let the family with the little girl go first. As soon as they set foot on solid ground, the girl turned to her mother. "Now?" she asked. When the woman nodded, the girl tossed her hands in the air, her fingertips crackling with what looked like lightning. Laughing indulgently, her father put a hand on her shoulder and ushered her up the steps and inside, nodding to the Kavanaghs as they passed.

By the time Eleanor and I got out of the gondola, the family were gone. "Did you see that?" I asked. "I thought kids didn't usually mix with adults."

"Like I told you," Ben replied. "We're not the only game in town. I don't know who they were."

Daniel squinted after them. "Could be Elementals, maybe? If so, you won't see their like too often. Outside of the Masquerade, that is," he added. "But I've never heard of them with children before, either – nor yet heard of an Elemental who could work lightning. Wonders never cease."

At the top of the steps, two massive, iron-studded wooden doors were propped open, flanked by a pair of hooded, masked figures, standing so still I almost took them for statues. They did not ask our names, or anything else, but I suspected that costume or not, an uninvited party crasher would not make it past them.

I had read in a guidebook that the exteriors of Venetian buildings did not always give an accurate picture of what they looked like inside: that was certainly true in this case. Inside the doors was a marble anteroom with delicate wrought-iron benches along the walls, and beyond that we came down a broad shallow staircase into a ballroom that could have been lifted from Versailles, all gilt and mirrors and crystal. The room was already thronged with people, with more arriving every moment. Some were dancing; I looked around to see where the music was coming from and had the slightly unsettling realization that there was a small orchestra of instruments playing in thin air, with no apparent human input.

"It's a huge place," Ben said, just behind me. "Explore where you like, but do keep your wits about you. And whatever you do," he added, looking particularly at Claire before sweeping his gaze around to take in the rest of us, "don't leave alone, nor yet with a stranger. We are small fish in this pond, and there are folk here with powers well beyond ours."

We walked down into the ballroom together, but in the increasingly crowded space, I got separated from the others. With Ben's warning in the back of my mind, I felt a little uneasy, and kept my eyes peeled for anyone I might recognize. Further down the room, a woman lowered her hand-held mask for a moment and I saw that it was Isabella, peering at me uncertainly. Having no wish to engage with her, I made my way through an open door and found myself in a dim conservatory, lush with exotic plants and lit with candles hovering in mid-air.

It was less crowded, but only slightly. Continuing on down the rabbit hole, I came into a long hallway, open on one side as a gallery to another ballroom below. The gallery ran around three sides of the chamber, and seemed an ideal spot from which to watch and get my bearings for a little while. Most of the women had decked themselves out in full Baroque extravagance: silks and satins with cinched waists and incredibly voluminous skirts. Some also wore intricate wigs or huge feathered headdresses – as did some of the men who were not wearing hats. Although I had felt like my own outfit was elaborate while putting it on, I realized that if anything I was somewhat underdressed for the occasion.

Across the gallery, also looking down at the dancers, I saw the little girl from the gondola; she noticed me at the same moment and gave me a wave, which I returned.

"Do you know her?" came a voice at my elbow.

I turned to see an elegant silver-haired gentleman who looked quite at home in his eighteenth-century garb. A little voice at the back of my mind wondered if that was because he actually came from that era. "No. We were in the same gondola coming here, and I was surprised to see a child."

"You would not be the only one," he replied, waving to her himself. His voice and manner of speaking made me think of a Shakespearean actor. "I doubt there has been a child at the Masquerade in centuries."

"Isn't it..." I trailed off, wondering how much I should say to a stranger. But he tilted his head and indicated for me to continue, so I resumed, cautiously. "It seems like this might not be the wisest place to bring a child."

"And you would be quite correct, if it were any ordinary child. That child, however, may well be the safest person here. Oh dear... If you will excuse me, there is someone I must speak to. Good evening."

I was opening my mouth to bid him good evening as well, but all that came out was a strangled gasp as the man hopped effortlessly up onto the railing and... fell? Jumped? Whatever he had done, he landed lightly as a feather, as if he had only dropped a couple of feet rather than twenty or so. A few heads turned at his unexpected descent, but only for a moment. It seemed I was the only one truly shocked by this little display.

That was the first real sign that I was out of my league, but there were many more to come. As I wandered around the huge palazzo over the course of the evening, I saw people walking up walls and across ceilings, a woman completely unperturbed by the fact that her hair was on fire, and more than one individual who could pass through solid objects. At one point I came face-to-face with a massive, snarling black bear, and was quickly disabused of my assumptions when it proved solid enough to knock me down with one swipe of its enormous paw. I screamed as it loomed over me, leaning down with every apparent intent to rip my throat out – only to find myself a laughingstock as the beast turned into a man, his stylized bear mask twisted into an unpleasant leer. He closed his hand on my throat for a moment before getting up and bowing to a trio of white-clad ladies.

Shaken, I began retracing my steps, hoping to find someone I knew. I managed to make my way back to the shadowy conservatory, but where I expected to find the doorway to the first ballroom there was only a mirror. Instead, off to the left there was a smaller archway, candlelight spilling out of it. Well-lit seemed reassuring; I went that way. To my profound relief, I discovered a scene that I could understand: recognizable magic being performed to an audience. Even better, I spied Molly among a cluster of ladies watching the show. When she noticed me approaching, she parted from the group and led me to a bench at the side of the room. "You look white as a sheet, love. Sit down, and tell me what's happened."

I recounted the tale of all I had seen so far. "I was okay, up until the bear," I concluded. "And then... I couldn't find the ballroom again."

She nodded. "The whole house is set up like that. The rooms don't really change, I don't think – it's just that someone's able to make the doorways come and go. If you're patient, they open up again. Try not to worry; just watch out for what's going on around you."

Although I was still unnerved, I had to admit that most of the Masquerade was fascinating. After sitting a while longer, I felt ready to explore further. I was sure there was more for me to see.

CHAPTER FOURTEEN

Even bearing in mind that the doorways were liable to change from time to time, I began to feel like the mansion went on forever – not unlike the endless trees of the Magician's Walk. By the time I found my way to a third ballroom, I gave up trying to guess what floor I was on or how large the footprint of the place must be. This room was darker than any I'd come across, with a deep blue ceiling and walls alight with some kind of luminescent stars. At one end of the room, food and wine were being served. I was just debating whether it would be wise to have a drink when I heard someone call my name.

"Heather, is that you?" It was Luke, unmasked. When I nodded, he breathed a sigh of relief. "Christ, it's good to see a familiar face. Come and sit down, will you? Oh, and watch out for those drinks."

I saw a certain irony in his warning, given that our first meeting had involved him trying to ply me with a deceptively strong beverage, but I poured myself a tumbler of water and followed him to an alcove off to one side.

"I know we're supposed to keep these on," he said, indicating his mask. "But I've just come from a room full of fire, and I'm roasting. Besides, you can't eat or anything. You were smart to get the half kind." He stuffed a meatball into his mouth, then reached to put the mask back on.

"Leave it off for a minute," I said. "It's good just to see somebody's actual face. What's the weirdest thing you've seen so far?"

Luke looked up at the ceiling. "I guess the room I was just in, with the lava – did you see that?" When I shook my head, he continued. "There were people… I might be using the word a bit loosely… but they just… walked right into the lava and treated it like it was water. Their clothes and everything turned into fire, or at least that's what it looked like."

I told him about the bear-man. "It makes our whole group seem a bit tame, doesn't it?"

"I don't know. I think we do alright. We're just not out to throw it in people's face that we can be scary, you know? We wouldn't sell so many tickets if we did."

"Or be as welcome in the villages."

He nodded. "Not that I don't think there's people with us who could do it, if they wanted. Johannes could probably give the bear bloke a run for his money, but he's far too polite. I do like the costumes, though. More on the ladies, of course," he added, with a grin that reminded me that he was not yet twenty. "Speaking of which, do you mind…?" Inclining his head towards a cluster of attractive young women, he reached for his mask.

"Go ahead," I said, laughing. "Just watch yourself."

Almost as soon as he had vanished into the crowd on the dance floor, another man came and sat down in my little alcove, appearing to be surprised to find anyone there. I suspected that his reaction might be a little premeditated, but without being able to see people's faces it was so hard to tell. The man wore a hooded red cloak over his black suit, and a gold mask without any further embellishment; all I could see of his face were his eyes, heavily lined with black makeup.

"A lady so lovely should not sit alone," he said, moving over on the bench, closer to me than I was quite comfortable with.

"I was just talking to my friend," I replied, hoping to catch a glimpse of Luke, but he was gone. "I'm fine, thank you."

"Shall we dance, then?"

On the point of politely refusing, I suddenly found myself strangely compelled to agree. By the time I thought it through, we were already on the dance floor. I did not have the first idea how to waltz – at least, I assumed that was the dance – but the stranger led me through the moves, taking advantage of the steps to bring our bodies into closer proximity than necessary. But somehow, each time I was about to push him away, or leave the dance floor entirely, I found myself deciding to allow it. It was as if…

And then my head cleared, like a thunderclap. *Sébastien.* He was long dead, of course, but my ancestor had been well known for his ability to manipulate people, to make them do what he wanted them to do. Mind tricks. This man must have a similar talent. Of course. Now that I was aware of it, I could almost see the push-pull happening in my own brain.

"I'm going to go find my friends now," I said, trying to extricate myself from his embrace.

This time I could hear the stranger's voice in my brain, not quite the same as his spoken one. *You don't want to do that.* Narrowing my eyes at him, I concentrated on the fact that I did, in fact, want to do exactly that. If I carried the genetic legacy of someone who had been so exceptionally skilled at getting into people's heads, I should have at least some ability to keep other people out of mine. *Screw you,* I mentally tagged on.

The stranger's eyes widened for a moment, then narrowed; his left hand moved from holding my right hand to clasping tightly around my wrist, and he stopped dancing. "Who are you?" he hissed.

"Let me go." I kept my voice as level as possible, but did not take any trouble to keep it down. He was bigger than me, and most probably stronger, but he was about to have a fight on his hands if he had thoughts about dragging me off somewhere. I found I couldn't quite compel him to release my wrist, but he wasn't doing anything else, either; we seemed to be at some kind of a standoff.

"No one says no to me." There was rage in his voice now, ice-cold. "No one."

"I think the lady just did." I hadn't realized that anyone else had noticed what was happening, but out of nowhere there was a man at my side, slipping in between myself and the stranger as if he were politely cutting in on the dance. In fact, he did take my hand and put his other arm round my waist and spin me off to a different area of the dance floor, all so neatly in time to the music that no one around batted an eye. I wasn't sure I was in the mood for any more dancing or any more strangers, even though this man was conducting himself with far more decorum – but on the other hand, I did not want to be alone just then either. The scene with the first man had unfolded so quickly, I hadn't had time to be frightened, but it was catching up. I was shaking like a leaf.

My dance partner squeezed my hand just a little. "It's all right, Heather."

Belatedly, my brain registered the fact that I knew this voice; it had just been some time since I'd heard it. Looking past the black suit, past the ornate mask of the Green Man that covered nearly all of his face, I knew the eyes, too. "Eric!"

I hadn't realized till that moment just how much I'd missed him, or how much I'd feared that he wouldn't come back.

Forgetting that we were in the middle of a formal ballroom, I hugged him so hard I might have knocked the wind out of him. That did turn a few heads, so I gestured off to the side of the room. "We should talk."

There was a curtain that I thought would lead to another secluded corner, but in fact it opened out onto an outdoor terrace. A few people stood by a railing at one side, but there was plenty of unoccupied space, a relief after the crowded rooms. "Have you seen anyone else?"

Eric shook his head. "Not yet. I came incognito tonight. I wasn't sure I was ready to dive back in, but a hand-lettered invite found me in Buffalo, with no address and no postage, so it seemed important. I wasn't ready for a… for the whole thing, right now. But I'm glad to see you."

I was doing this in all the wrong order. "Eric, I'm so sorry about your dad," I told him, my voice wavering a little.

"Thanks," he said automatically, head bowed. But then he looked up. "Wait. How did you know…?"

There was nothing I could say but the truth. "I… I met him. I took the Magician's Walk, and I met your dad. Not quite two weeks ago." I wouldn't have believed it if I were him, so I continued. "Your dad's name is John and he still wears his hair in a buzz cut like a soldier. His left pinky finger was missing." There were probably other ways I could have found these things out, I knew. "You talked to your dad in the hospital and told him everything. Told him you're a magician, what you can do. He's so proud of you, Eric," I added, swallowing hard against the lump in my throat.

At that revelation, he sat down abruptly on a stone bench, pulling his mask off. Head down, he covered his eyes with one hand. I gave him a few moments, then perched down beside him and untied my mask as well; it seemed wrong to still be wearing it under the circumstances. "He didn't want you to feel guilty – he said you're too hard on yourself, and that you maybe get that from him - and he wanted to make sure you had... people here who would look out for you." I kept my voice low, not necessarily expecting a response, but needing to convey the message I'd been entrusted with. "And it's true: you do. I know you're probably not ready to deal with it all yet, or even to have everyone know you're back..." An awful thought struck me. "You are back, though, aren't you? This isn't... you're not just here to say goodbye or something?"

"No." He said it immediately, but took a moment before he looked up. When he did, I could see the traces of tears on his face. "No," he repeated, his voice steadier. "I am back. Or coming back, or something. I might just... stay on the sidelines for a bit. I don't know. I'm not ready to see anybody else tonight. I wasn't sure I'd even recognize anyone, with these costumes, but I knew you – and when it looked like you were in some trouble there..."

"Thank you. It's not the first disturbing thing that's happened tonight, but that guy actually seemed dangerous; I don't know what I would have done."

"I've always got your back," he said, leaning in so that his shoulder nudged mine. "You know, except for when you travel overseas based on something I wrote on the back of a card and I don't even show up to meet you. I feel horrible about that, Heather; I'm really sorry."

I shook my head. "You made sure someone was there. You were in the middle of a crisis and you still thought to leave your phone with Claire just so that I could reach someone when I got to Ireland. If I got there. You didn't even know for sure I was coming, and you still looked out for me. I know you've got my back, and I've got yours. If you don't want anyone else to know you're here, I won't say a word. Just... don't disappear, alright?"

Eric shook his head. "I won't."

CHAPTER FIFTEEN

"Do you want to just get out of here?"

Eric and I were still sitting on the terrace, the noise of the Masquerade seeping out through the open doors. Until he asked the question, it hadn't occurred to me to just up and leave, despite the fact that I didn't really want to go back into the party after my experience in the ballroom. "You know what? I would love to," I replied. "I guess there'll just be a gondola to take us back?"

He shrugged. "Presumably. Only one way to find out."

I felt like I should tell the others I was going, but Eric had said that he wasn't ready for everyone to know that he was back – and I doubted I could find them in any case. Apart from my brief run-ins with Molly and Luke, and a glimpse of Isabella, I hadn't seen any of our troupe since we'd arrived. I was glad I'd written down the address of where we were staying and tucked it into a hidden pocket of my dress, along with the key, otherwise I might have been left wandering the streets of Venice.

We tied our masks back on and re-entered the ballroom. There was no sign of the man who had tried to manipulate my mind on the dance floor, but I was uncomfortably aware of just how easily someone could lose themselves in the crowd. I kept a hand on Eric's arm, lest we get separated. Eventually, with a few wrong turns, we stumbled upon the way to the main entrance. The big wooden doors were closed, but they swung open noiselessly as we approached. I could see the shape of a gondola just gliding away from the empty jetty; within a few seconds, another one approached. The journey back to the public square seemed quicker than the trip to the Masquerade had been, and it was with great relief that I set foot back on the ground and watched the boat disappear into the night.

"Do you think there's anything open – coffee, or something, at this hour?" I asked, looking around at the empty square.

Eric took his mask off. "I don't know. To be honest, I had expected to either stay at the party all night, or – more likely – leave early and just take the first water taxi to the airport. To London, not Buffalo," he added quickly. "I came from the States and stopped off at home and just planned to come down here for the night. I picked up the mask and stuff when I got here, and didn't really bring anything else. Stupid, I know. I didn't really think any of it through."

Putting my mask aside as well, I took a closer look at him; I hadn't noticed earlier that his outfit was a normal black suit with a black dress shirt, rather than the period costume most of the men had been wearing. "I'm staying with Claire and Eleanor," I said. "Look – don't take this the wrong way, but why don't we just go there? There's a fold-out couch in the living room, and we've got some tea and snacks and things, if you want to just hang out and talk, or if you need some sleep, or whatever. I know it'll mean letting them know you're here, but they won't tell anyone, I'm sure. Besides, you probably do need to get your phone back."

He thought about this for a moment, running a hand through his hair. "Honestly, I could use a place to crash. I'm not ready for a bunch of people, but they're probably either still at the party or already back and asleep… I don't even know. I'm so worn out at this point that I'm not thinking rationally."

"You've had too much to think about." Digging in my pocket, I found the address and eyed it, wishing I'd thought to also bring along a map. "Just crash with us. Assuming I can find the place again, that is."

Eric took the scrap of paper from me. "You're staying at Emilio's?"

"Sort of. It's a separate apartment, upstairs. I've got a key, so we can bypass Ben and the others, if you want. Do you know where it is?"

He nodded. "We can walk from here; it's actually not far."

Considering the roundabout journey we had taken to get to the Masquerade, I was surprised to find that it only took about twenty minutes to walk back. We didn't talk much on the way, but as we approached the correct street, he stopped at the corner. "I'm still going back to London in the morning, first thing. I can just walk you to the door and…"

"Eric, I get that you don't want a big fanfare, and that you're probably not ready to deal with telling everybody about your dad right now. But frankly, since you're finally here, I could use some company right now too. I would really feel better if you stuck around for a bit." If I was being quite truthful, I didn't really need him to do that for me, but I was beginning to notice that he looked as though he hadn't slept properly in days. "If I have to smuggle you out at dawn, I will smuggle you out at dawn. Although *that* might make people talk, you know."

It had the desired effect: he laughed, and gave in. "Fine. But let's be quiet on the way in; I see lights on."

There were windows illuminated downstairs, but none in the attic; Eleanor and Claire must still be at the masquerade ball. "Do you want tea, or something?" I asked. "Just give me a minute to change out of this ridiculous dress."

"I'm happy just to be somewhere quiet, honestly. You don't need to get me anything." He took off his suit jacket, and laid it over a chair. When I returned from getting changed, the kettle was on. "For the record, the dress was beautiful."

Feeling suddenly awkward, I busied myself with making tea. "So… will you come back when we go to our next stop?" I asked, bringing the two cups over to the little living room. "I don't even know where it is, but I suppose you do."

"It's my old stomping grounds. Germany. Near where I was born," he elaborated, sitting down next to me on the couch. "Where my mom met my dad. Both of them," he added, with a slightly pained smile.

"Have you been back there many times?"

"More than some other places, yeah. There's a few interesting spots within an hour or two, so it seems like every two or three years we wind up somewhere in that general vicinity around this time. This is place where my mom actually met Ben, though, and where I almost found them for the first time – a little town called Bad Dürkheim. It's a nice place, mostly forest and vineyards. Funny that that's where I'll be coming back to."

I pondered this. "And do you know when we go there? Ben did say he'd told you a whole list."

"He did. I wonder if he'd get in trouble if people knew that. We set up there on the fourth – Monday – which is why I have to head home tomorrow, to actually get prepared."

It made sense. Colleen had advised me to bring all my things to Venice, so I had assumed we would be going straight from there to our next stop. "Will you be okay?"

"I'm fine. But enough about me," he said, although in truth we hadn't talked very much about what had happened to him over the past several weeks. "How are you making out? Did they give you a hard time at Tara?"

"Nobody was at Tara. Apparently, it only lasted two days after you left."

He nodded. "I wondered about that. But Claire came and got you?"

I recounted how I had arrived, only to find myself installed as a guest at Fernwood. "They brought Manon from Belgium to give me a couple weeks of basically boot camp, and then it was off to Wéris and right into it. Luke convinced me to perform with him."

"What did you do?"

Knowing I wasn't articulating it terribly well, I tried to describe the act. "I still can't quite believe that I pulled it off."

"I believe it." He shook his head. "I'm so sorry I missed it. Your triumphant premiere."

I laughed. "That might be overstating it, but I guess it went okay. I wasn't expecting just how drained I would feel, though, or how much…" I bit my lip, not sure of what I was really trying to say.

"How much what?"

"How much… I don't know. How big a hole you left behind. Everyone missed you. I know I did," I added, after he made a slightly dismissive noise. "I was just always conscious of you not being there. I'm not saying that to make you feel guilty. I just… I don't want you to think that nobody cared you were gone." I was speaking faster, needing to articulate this somehow but feeling quite nervous at saying it aloud. "Especially since you'd just… gone. I kept wanting to tell you about what was happening, and get your thoughts on things, like at Callanish. So, I... I've been carrying these around."

Hands trembling a little, I pulled out the stack of magician's cards, all covered with notes in the smallest handwriting I could manage. "Every time I felt like I needed to talk to you, I wrote it down instead." I put them in his hand.

"Can I read these?"

"I wouldn't give them to you otherwise."

He stood up and walked away with them, pacing slowly around the room as he began to read. There was nothing particularly profound or personal – there wouldn't have been room to squeeze it into the little cards even if I'd wanted to. Just notes of the moments I'd experienced, questions or observations that I would have put to him without a second thought if he had been around. And so I was shocked when he turned back to me, tears in his eyes once again.

"Thank you," he said, folding me up in a tight hug.

"For what?"

"Just... being there, I guess," he replied, his voice slightly muffled. "It's been... the last few weeks have been really hard. The fact that you give a damn means a lot right now."

I wasn't the only one who gave a damn, and I knew that deep down he knew that too. But we were still standing in the middle of the room holding onto each other when we heard feet on the stairs a few seconds later. He immediately stepped away and sat back down on the couch, out of view of the entrance, hastily wiping the last trace of dampness from around his eyes and taking a sip of tea.

Intending to head Eleanor and Claire off at the entrance and give a quick explanation of his presence, I found that they were accompanied by Daniel and Ben. "She's here!" Claire exclaimed, the moment I opened the door.

"We've been worried sick," Ben admonished me, in a tone of voice I remembered my own dad having used in my teen years. "I said nobody should leave the party alone, and when we couldn't find you we heard you'd been seen leaving with a strange man. Are you alright? What were you thinking, going off without a word?"

I could see that they had all been concerned, and I owed a great deal to their hospitality; I felt like I should explain myself somehow, but I had also told Eric that I would keep his presence quiet. "I didn't go anywhere with a stranger," I faltered.

"More than one person said they saw you. Yes, she's here!" he shouted down the stairs. "Dad, go on down and tell Mum and Colleen that Heather's alright." Turning back towards me, he fixed me with a glare. "There were plenty of dangerous people at that ball. I know you're a grown woman, but you'd do well to heed my advice next time."

"There *were* dangerous people there," I retorted. "As a matter of fact, that was why I left."

"By yourself, then? That's scarcely better, at this hour in a place like this."

"She wasn't by herself." The voice came from behind me, and I felt Eric's hand on my shoulder. "She was with me. I'm really tired, and not ready to deal with explanations right now," he added. "We'll talk when we all meet in Germany, alright?"

Ben nodded, a very different look on his face. "Of course. Of course. I won't say a word. Welcome back, son."

Glancing back, I saw Eric flinch at the choice of words, but he nodded. "Thanks."

Ben departed, leaving Claire and Eleanor staring after Eric as he retreated to the couch and his cup of tea. "You didn't see him," I explained in an undertone. "He's not officially back yet – he'll be gone in the morning – but he'll join us all at the next stop."

Claire nodded, and went to exchange a brief greeting with her half-brother before retiring to bed. Eleanor, however, was giving me an odd look.

"It's not what you think," I said quietly.

She glanced in the direction of the living room, then back at me. "If you say so. Goodnight, Heather."

We talked a while longer after Claire and Eleanor turned in, but I could see that Eric was fading; I found a blanket and pillow, and helped him unfold the couch. "I have a feeling you'll be gone before I wake up, especially now that the cat's out of the bag," I mused.

"Guilty as charged. But just for a couple of days. I've got to pack like a sane person, and not go running off across several countries with just the clothes on my back," he said, gesturing to his dress shirt and trousers. "And just some stuff to take care of. Bills to pay, that sort of thing."

"Did Claire give you back your phone?"

"Yeah."

"Good." Pulling out one of the few blank magician's cards I had left, I wrote down my phone number – needing to check to make sure I had it correct before I handed it off to him. "Because I'm going to hold you to that not-disappearing thing."

I woke up to find the couch folded away, the pillow and blanket sitting tidily at one end serving as the only evidence that someone had been there. "He's gone back to his place in England for a couple of days," I explained to Claire and Eleanor when they emerged. "They delivered a masquerade invite all the way to Buffalo, so he came to see what it was about."

"What happened with his father?" Claire asked.

I shook my head. "He passed away. I don't think he's ready to talk about it yet."

Claire bent her head and crossed herself. "Old habits die hard," she said, in response to my surprised look. "I was afraid of that, with how he looked last night. I'd better go and tell Dad. He won't tell anyone else," she added, "but after everything last night, he's probably said something to Gran and Granddad – and Mum. I'll just go and have a word so they know not to say the wrong thing when we get to Germany."

"Germany, is it?" Eleanor said, as Claire left the room. "I figured it was about that time. Now tell me, honestly, what happened last night? I know, I know – nothing like that. You don't have to tell me again. But... Right. The poor bloke comes back from a death in the family, and needs to take some time out of the limelight to deal with it. That much I understand, especially with the whole adopted dad, biological dad thing. That's not a secret," she added. "And for a lot of people here, he's Ben's son, full stop, and some of them may not entirely get it. And yeah, *maybe* he came to the Masquerade just to see what it was about, and to be a spectator on the sidelines. But I saw you from down the hall or across the room at least three times last night, and every time there was this man in a Green Man mask shadowing you. I had no idea who it was – that was half the reason we were all so worried last night – but it doesn't sound like an accident that you were the one he bumped into."

I exhaled heavily. "I don't know. You'd have to ask him, and now is probably not the time." My tone was sharper than I meant it to be, and I tried to moderate it. "All I know is that I got stuck on a dance floor with a creepy mind-controlling dude who wasn't too happy that I could say no to the suggestions he was trying to put into my head. I didn't even recognize Eric until about two minutes after he got me away from the guy. After that, I was only too happy to take off. I'm sorry if I worried everyone, but I honestly hardly saw a familiar face all night."

"I know, I know. It's alright," she said, reaching up to pat down the cowlick I sometimes woke up with. "And between his dad, and your ex, and everything else… I'm not trying to be a busybody."

"Then what?"

"Just… keep an open mind, I guess. I know you're fond of him, he clearly feels the same, and frankly, it's hard enough to find a decent person out there in the regular world, let alone the whole magician thing. If I'm wrong, and you just wind up staying as great friends, that's a fine thing to have too, mind you."

"I'm finding more great friends here than I think I ever had in the 'regular world'," I replied, reaching across the counter to squeeze her hand. "Clearly I must be in the right place."

CHAPTER SIXTEEN

"I know we're all night people, but this is ridiculous."

This time, the older generation had taken the option of travelling in the vans. The reason, as I soon learned, was that there was no particularly quick public transit option between Venice and Bad Dürkheim. Hence I found myself blinking wearily at the clock on the train platform at Venezia Mestre station: it read one-fifteen in the morning. Shouldering my backpack, I followed Eleanor aboard the train, the first of many connections that we would need to get to our destination.

Several travellers were already aboard, most of them young backpackers at this time of night. I spotted Luke, but he was already sharing a bank of four seats with Gavin, Tom and another man whose name I didn't know. "Where's Claire?" he asked, as we passed.

"She's squeezing in the van with her mum and dad," Eleanor replied. "We'll see you later?"

We had to continue down into the next car to get seats together. I was surprised that so many people travelled in the dead of night, but then again I supposed for some it would save a night's accommodation. "Breakfast in Austria," Eleanor reminded me. "Delicious pastries. I'm going to try to grab some sleep till then."

In our short acquaintance, I had already noticed her enviable ability to fall asleep in minimal time in practically any circumstances; this was no different. By the time the train pulled out of the station some fifteen minutes later, she was already dozing. I watched the lights pass by the carriage windows for a while, but soon we were into the countryside with nothing to see at all, not even moonlight.

On impulse, I pulled out my phone and texted Eric, hitting send before I could dither about it. *Fifteen hours to Bad Dürkheim. Too bad nobody's figured out a better way to do this.*

I didn't expect a response, particularly at that hour. Really, it was not so different from scratching out my thoughts on a card – although it did occur to me to hope that he didn't have a notification tone that would wake him up.

However, a few minutes later: *Fifteen hours – how are you getting there, camel and balloon?*

Train. Make that trains, plural, I replied.

That can't be right. Train from London is taking me 7.5 hours in the morning. It's got to be the same distance?

High-speed trains in France for you, though, I sent back. *And probably no 3-hr stopovers. Eleanor promised breakfast in Austria, think it will be at 4am.*

There was a pause, long enough that I thought he might have stopped responding. If he was taking the train down in the morning, he certainly had better things to do than texting me in the wee hours of the night.

We must get there around the same time. 4pm?

4:30, I think, I replied. *We're all supposed to be meeting up at some restaurant at 6.*

Ok. There's a café not far from train stn. Coffee (Beer? Ice cream?) in it for you.

I smiled at the screen. *Might be cold for ice cream, no? You should get some sleep. Will text when we get in.*

We piled off the train at Villach, just inside the Austrian border, a little past four in the morning. Our onward train to Salzburg didn't depart till after seven, so it did indeed seem as though this was our best chance for breakfast. Nothing in the station was open, but Luke and Gavin led us on a search until we found a bakery that was just rolling up its shutters to start the day. Fortified with coffee and a paper sack full of assorted strudels and croissants, we took our time wandering back to the station through the barely-awakening streets.

"What did you think of the Masquerade in the end, Heather?" Gavin asked.

"I don't know. The parts that were good were fascinating, and the parts that were bad were pretty awful. I'm glad I went, but I don't feel any burning need to go again, that's for sure."

Luke leaned in, brushing crumbs off his sweater as he talked through a mouthful of something. "Who do you reckon some of those people were? I didn't know for sure there was anyone else, besides the lot of us. I mean, I figured there kind of had to be," he added, amid protests from the others. "But nobody ever talks about it."

"Well, it's not like we talk about anything we do, to anybody else," Eleanor pointed out. "Apart from handing out cards."

There followed a lively debate about the possible nature and numbers of other magical people in the world, but I tuned it out after a while. I still felt like I'd barely scratched the surface with the magicians I actually knew personally.

The rest of the train connections had only ten minutes or so in between – just enough time to find the platforms we needed – and so lunch fell by the wayside, apart from a bottle of water and a chocolate bar I had stashed in my bag. By the time we were approaching Bad Dürkheim in the late afternoon, I was somewhat light-headed from hunger; from the sounds of the complaints, most of my travelling companions were feeling much the same way. A plan was being hatched to go straight to the restaurant for an early dinner, but I excused myself, saying I had an errand to run.

"What errand?" Eleanor asked. I gave her a pointed look, at which she nodded. It was time to start collecting our bags and getting ready to leave the train, so she took advantage of the commotion to speak to me more quietly. "If he thinks it's going to be low-key to walk into the bar unexpectedly with everyone there, he's thought wrong."

I nodded. "I think that's why he asked me to meet him first."

At the station, I let them go on ahead while I picked up a local map to get my bearings. *Forget coffee, I'll take a sandwich,* I texted to Eric. *Be there in 5, as long as I don't get lost.*

As it happened, the café was only about a hundred metres away from the train station, once I got pointed in the right direction. Walking up to it, I could see Eric through the plate-glass windows, looking at his phone; I heard a beep from mine as I walked in the door. "Make it two minutes," I said, walking up to the table and setting my backpack down on the floor.

"I was just texting you directions. I can't believe you had to take fifteen hours' worth of trains." He stuck his phone back in his pocket and stood up to give me a hug. "Let me grab you something to eat. What do you want?"

There was a menu chalked up on a board by the counter, but my German was sketchy at best. "Anything. Ham sandwich, cheese, whatever they've got."

He came back a few minutes later with two ham sandwiches, two beers and a bottle of water. "I'd better have the water first," I told him, laughing. "That'd go right to my head." After wolfing down half the sandwich, I began to feel a little more like myself. "Thank you; I was about to fall over. How are you doing?"

"About as well as can be expected, I guess. Part of me is glad to be back, but part of me is still finding it all pretty surreal. I think it'll be better after tomorrow's out of the way – get the first night under my belt, deal with everybody and get back to it, you know?"

"Are you coming to the thing tonight?"

He sighed. "I might as well. There won't be as many people there, since half of them won't get here till the morning. And I should see Ben, especially after the other night. I'm sorry I put you in an awkward position there."

"It wasn't awkward. Well, not very. Honestly, I'm just glad you're back."

"Look, about that. No, no, I'm not going anywhere," he said hastily, seeing my expression. "But I need your help with something."

"Of course. What is it?"

He took a long sip of his beer. "Will you perform with me?"

I looked at him, open-mouthed. "Seriously?"

"I mean, if you didn't have plans with Luke already…"

"No. No plans, but…" I held my palms up. "You're amazing, and I can barely do anything yet. How could I possibly help you?"

"You know what they say: two heads are better than one." He lowered his voice a little. "I just… I could use some help to stay focused. I'm not sleeping much, still."

Indeed, I could see the dark circles under his eyes. "If you think I can help, I'm happy to do it."

He smiled, then, and clinked his beer bottle against mine by way of agreement. But I had barely taken a sip before we were both startled by a rap on the window outside. Gavin stood there, astonished, gesturing at Eric.

Eric rolled his eyes and quickly drained the rest of his drink. "Cat's right out of the bag now, I guess. Shall we go and face the music?"

Gavin didn't ask too many questions, just led the way down a couple of narrow side streets to a little restaurant that looked like it had been around forever. It was a tiny place, and the thirty or so magicians sitting inside made the room almost crowded despite the fact that it was otherwise closed to the public. Only a few pairs of eyes glanced up when we entered, and none of them seemed unduly startled by Eric's presence. It was only in seeing his shoulders loosen up at this that I realized he'd been braced for some kind of a scene.

Ben got up immediately from his table in the corner. "I'm so sorry to hear about your dad, Eric." He shook his hand, then hugged him. "We'd all hoped for different news. How's your mum doing?"

Eric took a breath. "She's alright, under the circumstances. My brother and sister are there to help."

"I'd like to send her my condolences, but I'll leave that in your hands, if you think it would be right," Ben added. "But it's good to see you back. Come in and have a drink, and some dinner."

We joined him at a long table and were soon plied with food and drink by the proprietor. Most of the talk was focused on the practicalities of the show, which would start the next night; after the strangeness of Venice, this felt almost normal, which was a huge relief. The carnival would be set up just outside the town, on the fringes of a forest, since there were few truly open fields in the vicinity that weren't given over to vineyards. I privately wondered whether there was some convenient magical way to keep the tents heated, since we were well into the first week of November and the nights were certain to get colder, but I resolved to put that question to someone later.

The issue of where everyone would stay was also a priority. A woman named Claudia, who I had seen around but not met personally, pulled a steno notebook from her purse, flipped it open and began listing off names, rather like a roll call at school. Most people simply nodded, clearly already aware of their plans, while a few asked her for addresses and details. My name came up right after the Kavanaghs. "Heather will…"

"Actually," Eric put in. "Annika's got room for a couple extra. Heather can stay there. Eleanor too – unless you had other plans?"

Eleanor looked his way from a few spaces further up the table. "Fine by me."

Claudia shrugged and drew a couple of lines through her list, then carried on. I turned to Eric. "Who's Annika?"

"Family friend, actually. Both ways. The first time I came back to this neck of the woods, after joining, she let a few of us stay in the loft of her old barn. When she found out I was American, and what my name was, it turns out she knew my mom, back when I was a baby. They lost touch when we moved back to the States, but here it is: small world. I always stay there when we come through here. Not in the barn anymore," he added.

After dinner, the three of us shouldered our bags once more. Annika's house was just outside the main built-up area, a short walk up the wooded hill that loomed large over the little town. Set back from the road, inside a walled garden, it was a friendly-looking place, white with green shutters and a tiled roof. Our host was peering out the front window as we came in the gate, and immediately came to open the front door.

"Eric! I was wondering when you would arrive. Come in, come in. Who are your friends? I know you, I think," she added, shaking hands with Eleanor.

Once proper introductions had been made, and Annika had been assured repeatedly that we'd already had dinner, she showed Eleanor and me to a ground-floor room with a pair of twin beds. "The sunshine is quite bright in the early morning, but there is a blind," she pointed out. "My room is upstairs and very quiet, so do not worry that you would disturb me; I know that you all keep very late nights."

After we had settled in a bit, Annika called us back to the dining room table, where she had brought out snacks – despite our protests that we were all quite full – and a bottle of red wine. "Now, tell me of your travels," she asked.

We exchanged looks for a moment, before Eleanor began by telling a bit about my first performance at Wéris, which led to several questions from Annika about how I had come to join the group. We all managed to skirt around the Masquerade, and I noticed that Eric was mentioning nothing about his absence, so we avoided that as well. Eventually, when the older woman had excused herself to bed, Eleanor turned and regarded Eric and me. "Now, honestly. Am I just here to act as your chaperone so that people don't talk?"

I didn't know what to say to that – although I found myself blushing for no good reason – but Eric laughed, and picked up her hand across the table and kissed it. "You know I love you, El. And I needed some friends I can talk to."

"And...?"

"And yes, you're here to protect Heather's good name. You know how people are. This bunch in particular."

A little later, after Eleanor had called it a night, his expression turned more serious. "I do love Eleanor, but she's not wrong. I'm sorry if I put you on the spot about staying here."

I shrugged. "I seem to recall you staying the night to make sure I was alright at Callanish, the night Raffaele died. People are going to say whatever they're going to say." It was only a little after ten-thirty, but I had been up for close to twenty-four hours and had not slept on the train; details seemed unimportant. "I've got to go to bed or I'll be useless tomorrow. Good night, Eric."

He stood up from the table and patted my shoulder. "Good night."

CHAPTER SEVENTEEN

In the secluded yard behind Annika's house, a swarm of wispy, glowing dragonflies was circling. "Okay, change... now," Eric instructed, and their forms merged, becoming a flock of ravens. "Steady..."

Concentrating harder, I tried to focus light into tiny spheres to approximate eyes for the birds. I knew it was his skill, far more than mine, that was keeping things together, but he was smiling.

"Let it go if you need a break," he said.

"Maybe just for a minute." I stepped back, shaking my hands out, and he let the birds fizzle into a cloud and blow away. "I think it's going to be okay, right?"

"It's going to be great." He wrapped his arms around me for a moment. "This is the first thing I've felt positive about since I got to Tara, I think. Thanks, Heather."

"Hell, I just hope I don't cramp your style too much." I still wasn't sure how I was helping, but it was clear that something was; throwing an act together at the last minute, he had lost the haunted look that had been hanging about him since his return.

"You won't. I'll let you be the judge of when we need to stop. It's getting late, though," he added, looking down the hill at the shadow spreading over the town. "We should go."

The nights were closing in. To get the tents set up and ready in time, we had to walk down just after three in the afternoon; dark would fall no later than five. It was a very different picture, seeing the tents rising in clearings and under trees. Strategy was needed in order to keep the largest open spaces for the ones that would need it most: the red-and-gold striped Menagerie and the big purple marquee that housed magicians' gatherings as well as performances. For ourselves, we hoisted a tent beneath the branches of a massive beech tree, and coloured the silks silver-grey.

The season was not yet late enough to threaten frost, but it would be cold after dark. As the lights flickered on, I received the answer to my wonderings about warmth: scattered around the grounds were pillars, each topped with a shallow dish filled with something that looked like flame, and gave heat like flame, but did not actually burn. From the Feast tent the smells of apple cider, fried dough, and mulled wine began to waft past as the first patrons wandered under the trees.

We performed early, wanting to jump in while the afternoon's practice was still fresh. The tent was perhaps three-quarters full, and the act went off successfully – though I suspected that Eric could have carried on far longer if I had been able to. Afterwards, Ben caught up with us as we stood warming our backs by one of the braziers. "Can I have a word?"

He and Eric walked a few paces away, their heads bent close together. The conversation was brief, and Eric strode off into the night, head bowed.

I chased after Ben. "What was that about?"

"I'm sorry I didn't tell you earlier, darling, but it's taken most of today to pull things together. We'll wind things up a little early tonight, midnight or so, and then we'll gather in the big tent and have a proper wake for John Heyward."

"But... none of you knew him."

Ben shook his head. "It doesn't matter. We know Eric, and he's lost his father, and he shouldn't be alone with that. I know he thinks he is." He looked off into the direction that Eric had gone. "It's the right thing to do."

I wondered if Eric agreed with that assessment.

It took a good twenty minutes or so of wandering the aisles of tents – making wrong turns here and there, despite having helped to set most of them up – before I found him. In fact, I nearly tripped over him, sitting in the sparse grass between one tent and another. "Are you alright? Ben's just told me."

He looked up. "I think so."

"You don't sound so sure." Then I thought of Callanish. "Where are the stones here? Or whatever it is that we're here for?" In all the rush of travel, and then trying to put an act together, I had somehow spent twenty-four hours in Bad Dürkheim without remembering to ask anyone what the significance of the town might be to us, never mind visiting the site to prepare for our performance. No wonder I'd only been able to carry on for a few minutes.

"The wall?"

"It's a wall?" I replied, momentarily distracted.

"Some kind of Celtic fort. Around the top of the hill. There's trails going up." He was clearly puzzled, but he did get to his feet.

"Can you show me? Now?"

"I see what you're doing," he said. "Go to the stones, you'll feel better."

He didn't seem particularly disposed to go anywhere, so I pulled him by the hand. "I'm not saying it's going to instantly make everything alright; I'm not an idiot. But it might help clear your head."

There was just a sliver of a moon, but the stars were bright as we made our way down the road and found the hiking trail leading up the hill. Once we started to ascend and the trees closed in, though, it got very dark indeed. I hoped I wasn't pulling a foolish stunt that would end with one of us getting an ankle broken. After about fifteen minutes, I thought I could feel something up ahead. "Cast some light," Eric said. "There's no one around to know."

Following his example, I conjured up a small amount of light in the air, just enough to see what seemed to be a very rough stone path cutting a straight line away through the forest.

"This is it: the Heathen Wall. Just watch your step."

The stones were uneven, ranging from the size of my foot to the size of my head. At one point I did lose my balance – and with it, my wisp of light - but Eric caught me by the arm before I could fall. "I'm sorry; when you said a 'wall' I imagined something we could sit down and lean against, like the stones at Callanish."

"It's okay." He crouched down, his light disappearing as well as he extended his hands to feel the stones below. It took several moments for my eyes to adjust to the greater darkness; his white shirt was the main thing distinguishing him from the forest around us. "You were right. This is helping."

I put my hands down to the rocks. The energy was different yet again from what I had experienced elsewhere; I might have been reading into it because it was called a wall, but it felt solid, heavy, something welling up slowly from the earth rather than connecting me into a current. "You're going to go, aren't you?" I asked, spreading out my hands on a particularly smooth stone. "To the wake. I know it probably feels weird, and they didn't give you much warning, but they want to do this for you."

"I know. And it won't be a huge thing, just a few friends. I just need to think of what I want to say, and whether I'm going to be able to keep it together. The actual funeral was really hard."

Cautiously, I sat down, needing to give my knees a break. "I can imagine."

"Maybe not. I didn't tell you everything that happened. I told you that my parents told me about the adoption thing on my twenty-first birthday, right?" Without waiting for an answer, he continued. "Well… they never told my brother and sister. They're younger; they were only sixteen and fourteen at the time. And I just… I never told them myself; I didn't want them to think badly of my mom, and by the time we were all old enough that it wouldn't have mattered, I was over here."

"And you told them now?"

"I didn't. An old school friend did. I don't know exactly what got said, but somehow, it came out right before the funeral. Trevor and Dawn – especially Dawn – have always kind of felt like I deserted the family by being so far away, and now they know I'm not even my father's son."

Reaching out in the dark, I found his hand splayed out on a rock; I put mine over it. "I'm sure they were just in shock. You all must have been. They'll come around. And even if they don't," I added, more quietly, "as far as your dad was concerned, you're definitely his son. He made that pretty clear."

Eric made a noise of assent, then asked if I would give him a minute. Bringing back the light – much easier now, with the energy from the wall – I got to my feet and carefully picked my way back to the main trail. He rejoined me perhaps five minutes later. "Let's go. It must be almost time."

When we got back to the tents, the show was indeed winding down, the grounds nearly empty. The braziers had been extinguished, leaving a faint smell of something like candle wax in the air. Only the purple tent had a light still inside, and there was a magician standing guard lest the few remaining onlookers try to wander in. He stood aside for us, and we stepped over the threshold to find the space inside nearly filled.

Eric stopped short. "Everyone... Everyone is here," he said, his voice barely audible.

"Of course they are," I replied. "They love you."

He swallowed hard, and stepped forward to accept the condolences of his fellow magicians. The atmosphere was more sombre than Raffaele's wake had been; passing at the age of seventy-nine was considered very young by those who had spent their lives surrounded by magic. Overall, though, it was not as heavy as a traditional funeral, and there was plenty of food and drink to go around. It reminded me a little of the 'celebration of life' that had been held for my Granny Chrissie's passing.

After a while, Eric made his way to one end of the tent and climbed on top of one of the long tables. Almost immediately, the room fell silent. "I... I wasn't expecting anything like this. None of you knew my dad, so I'd like to tell you a couple of things about him." He paused. "John Heyward – my father – was a guy who always asked himself what he could do for other people. He went into the United States Air Force right out of high school because he wanted to fly planes, and he wanted to serve his country. He just missed the end of the Korean War, and a couple of years later got stationed at Ramstein, not too far from where we are right now. He eventually saw combat in Vietnam, then came home to Buffalo injured, but in one piece - almost. He lost a finger, which I thought was pretty cool when I was a little kid. When he came home, he worked a lot, but always had time for me, and my brother and sister. He never missed a game, or a school play, or whatever other little things we were into."

The room was completely quiet for a moment as he paused. "When I grew up and moved away, he was my biggest supporter; never questioned what I felt I had to do, even though he never got the whole story of what that was. He was a guy who loved his family, loved his hometown, loved a cold beer and a steak on the barbecue and a good hockey game. Probably in that order – although sometimes during hockey season we weren't always sure," he added, drawing a few chuckles from the listening crowd.

"That's the version that I would tell to anyone. But you're not just anyone," he continued, looking around the room. "There's more to the story, as I think you all know. My dad met a girl at Ramstein, a young nurse who was working there as a way to have an adventure and see the world. He fell for her right away, he told me once, even though everyone told him she didn't date enlisted men. But he hung around anyways, even when rumour had it she'd met some Irish guy." Several sets of eyes turned towards Ben, who acknowledged it with a nod. "When it seemed they'd parted ways, he thought, 'here's my chance'. Except that she told him she was pregnant. Now, in nineteen-sixty that would have sent a lot of men running in the other direction, but not my dad. The way both of them told it, he got down on one knee almost before she finished the sentence, and said that he'd walk down to the chaplain's office and marry her that afternoon, if she'd have him. He raised me exactly as if I were his own flesh and blood, and not once – not once – did he treat me as anything less. And when he found out, at the end, that I'd reconnected with my..." His voice faltered. "With my roots, here, he was nothing but happy for me. I hope, wherever he is now, he's looking down on us and seeing that he doesn't need to worry." Reaching down, he picked up the glass that someone offered him. "Thanks for everything, Dad."

Glasses were raised all around the room, joining in the toast. "And thanks to all of you," Eric added, when a hush fell over the group again. "For being here for me tonight, and for the last twenty-five years. I always felt like the two halves of my life were completely separate, but they feel less like that today. You've all made me a part of this family, and for that I can't thank you enough." His voice wavered a little and he paused to take a sip of his drink. "Most people in the world are lucky if they have one family that gives a damn about them, and I have two. And... And most people would thank their lucky stars to have a father who looks out for them at every turn, teaches them what they need to know to have a good life, and welcomes them back no matter what they do. I have two." Stepping down from the table, he walked the few steps to where Ben stood. "Thank you."

There was another round of raised glasses and calls of "Hear, hear," as the two men embraced. I supposed that many of the magicians – the ones born into this, who didn't have to split their lives in two – might have privately thought that this acknowledgement was long overdue, but it didn't show on any of the faces that I could see. A whole group had already surrounded Eric, offering their condolences and support, leaning in to ask more about this man that none of them had ever known.

"Ben won't have expected that," came a voice just behind my shoulder. Turning around, I saw Daniel there.

"I thought you were going back to Ireland?"

He nodded. "We are, darling, we are. Germany in November is a little cold for the old bones to be out all night nowadays. But we wanted to be here tonight, once Ben told us what he'd planned. Eric's lost his dad, and besides, we don't get to see him so often as we'd like. Although..."

Daniel nodded his head, prompting me to look at who was talking to Eric. It was Colleen. We both edged a little closer to try to hear what was being said. In fact, it sounded like he was relating some kind of anecdote about trying to get to a hockey game in a snowstorm; I couldn't quite catch it all, but Colleen laughed here and there and it all seemed surprisingly cordial. I did hear what she said at the end, though: "Do come and see us at Fernwood, any time."

After she moved away, it was Daniel and Molly's turn to have a rare chat with their grandson. Reassured that he was okay, I gave them some space and went off to find a drink and a place to sit down. After a little while, Claire came and found me. "I wish I'd met his other family," she said, examining her half-empty glass.

"Who knows? I mean, his mum and siblings are still around. It might happen one day."

She twisted her mouth. "I kind of doubt it."

"You're probably right," I acknowledged. "But it seems like he's finally realized he's part of the family here too. I saw your mum talking to him. An actual conversation, and she invited him to Fernwood."

Claire nodded. "I saw that. A thawing of the cold war. I mean, they're never going to be pals, but if it means he can visit once in a while, I'll take it. What about you?"

"What about me?" I asked.

"Don't worry; I'm not Eleanor," she replied immediately. "I'm not asking what's going on between you. I've had enough people making assumptions about me and my mates, just because they happen to be men. But I feel like you're the friend he needs right now."

I nodded. "I saw his dad, you know." Briefly, I related what had happened on the Magician's Walk. "I don't know if it's that I started out a bit as Eric's project – he saw that I had a link to you

135

guys before I had any idea of it – so he feels responsible for me, but it seems like our paths are linked. He's already done a hell of a lot for me, so if I can do anything for him, I'm happy to. It's the least I can do."

CHAPTER EIGHTEEN

Sometime into the small hours of the morning, I finally saw Eric standing by himself. "How are you doing?"

He thought for a moment. "Drunk, actually, I think. Everyone who's come to talk to me about my dad has put a beer or a whisky or something into my hand."

Now that he mentioned it, I realized that he was swaying ever so slightly. "But okay, apart from that?"

"Yeah. Yeah, I am. I think this was the sendoff I needed to give him. We couldn't... we couldn't do this at home. Everyone was too much in shock still. I wasn't expecting any of this," he added, gesturing around at the tent, still half-full of people milling about. "It's funny, you know – Ben setting all this up, not expecting any thank-you or anything for it, just because he felt like it was the right thing to do... it's exactly what my dad would have done. They're a lot alike."

"It's not that funny, really," I countered. "Your mom loved them both, right?"

He nodded, swiping a hand across his eyes again, looking like words escaped him. I took him by the arm. "Come on, I think you're probably ready to call it a night." I wanted to find our way back to Annika's before either alcohol or exhaustion caught up with him. He was more intoxicated than he'd seemed at first, alternating between long silences and cracking bad jokes as we made our way slowly up the hill. At the house, he seemed to forget the gate was there, and nearly fell headlong over it into the bushes.

"I'm sorry, I'm a terrible drunk," he said, as I steadied him with one arm and opened the gate with my free hand. "I don't do this very often any more. Can we sit for a second? Get some fresh air before we go in?"

Making sure he was actually sitting on the garden bench and not tripping over it, I ducked inside and retrieved a bottle of water from the fridge. "Here, you could probably use this."

"Thanks." He tipped his head back and drank the whole thing, almost without taking a breath. "I used to do this too often. Stasia and I drank a lot. Think it was the only way we could stand each other. We got along great when we were drunk. Next morning, not so much."

I raised an eyebrow. The only time I'd actually met Stasia had been the night that Raffaele died; since then, I had only seen her in passing once or twice. Eleanor had mentioned her history with Eric, but I found I couldn't quite picture it. "Were you together long?"

"Um..." He tilted his head back and thought about it. "Nine years, almost ten? Something like that. A long time. We were basically married, for all intents and purposes. Long time ago, though. One of those young and stupid things, and then it sort of stuck. We didn't actually get along at all, except for... Sorry, I'm rambling. I do that when I'm drunk, too. Are you staying around?"

I blinked at the non-sequitur. "What, right now?"

"No, I mean with us. Are you going to move over here somewhere, travel with us all the time? Ben knows a guy in London who can work around the immigration stuff for you. You don't have to, you know, go and marry somebody to stay in the country or anything."

"I'm okay, actually. There's a way I can work it to stay in the UK. I'm certainly not in a rush to get married again anytime soon, even if it is just a marriage of convenience," I joked. "I'm going to go home at Christmas, I think, and get that paperwork started."

He smiled, a bit crookedly. "So you are staying."

"Yeah. I needed to try it a bit first, to be sure I wasn't completely useless."

"And to make sure we were actually there. I'm sorry I wasn't."

"Stop apologizing for that," I told him. "If you had bailed on your dad just to hang around and wait for me, I would have had to kick your ass."

Eric put one arm around my shoulders. "You're right. You're always right. You're an amazing magician, you know."

I ducked out from under his arm and hauled him to his feet. "Okay, you're definitely smashed. You'd better go to bed, before you say something really ridiculous."

He let me propel him into the house; once inside, he lay down on his bed with all his clothes still on, and almost immediately started to snore. I pulled his shoes off, left another bottle of water on the bedside table, and retreated to my room, where Eleanor was already asleep. Finally, around five in the morning, I closed my eyes.

I woke up just before eleven and found the house still quiet; a note from Annika said that she had gone to the post office but to help ourselves to whatever we liked. The mention of her errand reminded me that I hadn't checked my email in days. Retrieving my phone, I sat down at the table with a bowl of muesli and a glass of juice and deleted the junk until I was left with only a few messages worth reading.

The first was from my dad. *Got your letter. Nice to get something in the mailbox that's not a bill, and glad to hear you're having a good time,* he wrote. *Your mum and Lisa have been wondering how long you're planning to stretch out the vacation, or if you're looking for work there.*

I sighed. There would have to be some kind of explanation to offer them, one way or the other. How could I put it without constructing too ridiculous a lie – and considering that the truth was fundamentally unbelievable? I skimmed down the rest of the message – updates about what the rest of the family were up to – and was about to close it when I noticed a postscript. *You might be hearing from Alan. Your mum bumped into him when she was in Toronto last week, and he was asking after you. She said he seemed upset when he heard you'd gone to Europe.*

Closing the message, I rolled my eyes and shook my head.

"What's wrong?"

I looked up from my phone to see Eric in the doorway, one hand to his head, looking decidedly ragged round the edges. "Ugh. Nothing. Supposedly my ex is heartbroken that I've moved away," I replied, taking no trouble to hide my sarcasm. "But to hell with him. Are you up for some breakfast?"

Eric didn't mention it again until later. We were out in the yard, practising – or attempting to. "I'm sorry," he said. "I might need to take a pass on tonight. My head feels like the inside of a pinball machine."

"I'm not surprised. But I think you're allowed, under the circumstances. Why don't we just go and watch tonight?" It was a warmer day, and I sat down in a patch of sunshine on the grass.

He sat down as well, and looked over at me, his brow furrowed. "Your ex-husband; I didn't realize that was so recent."

"I guess you don't have to be all that young to be stupid," I replied.

"Was he... really bad?"

"Yes and no." I pushed a stray piece of hair out of my face as the breeze picked up. "The whole time we were together he seemed great. I only found out at the end that he'd been cheating on me, with anyone who so much as batted their eyes in his direction. I never would have believed that I could be fooled so badly. The sort of thing that makes you question whether you can ever trust anybody again."

He summoned up a small bird shape of grey mist and sent it flying around me before it blew away. "And did you come up with an answer to that question?"

Watching the last of the illusion disperse, I smiled. "I'm working on it."

CHAPTER NINETEEN

We had been in Germany just over a week when Eleanor caught up with me one night outside the Menagerie. "Heather, you need to come with me for a second."

There was something in her tone that prevented me from asking any questions until we arrived at the tent where she based her security work. It was a mottled pattern, not unlike military camouflage, and blended in with the edge of the forest; I had never been inside before. There was something shimmering in midair when we stepped in, rather like a large transparent display screen, with a shifting pattern of coloured dots on it. "What is this?"

A stocky man with olive skin and an unruly mop of black hair emerged from behind the illusion. "A map of the grounds," he said. "And everyone in it."

"Heather, Ari; Ari, Heather," Eleanor said, by way of introduction.

"And you guys do this?" As I studied it more closely, I could just make out the outlines of the tents.

"Among other things," Eleanor replied. "It's a bit radar, a bit Harry Potter, but I take the ideas where I find them. The white dots are visitors; the blue ones are our people."

I noticed something else, though, in one corner of the map. "What about this red one?"

She put her finger almost on it, tracing its movements. "That's the thing. It's someone else. Not normal, not us. We sometimes get green dots; that's when someone turns up who has latent magical ability, whether they know it or not. Such as when you came to Callanish. We keep an eye on them; most of the time they just go about their business and we don't get involved."

There was one thing about colour codes, in my experience, that rarely varied. "And red means danger."

Ari tilted his head. "Not always. But it's someone with magic – a practitioner – who we don't know. Could be harmless, especially this soon after Venice; could just be someone who met one of us at the Masquerade and is coming by for a visit. Or could be… who knows. Either way, we spot a red dot, we send Markus out to investigate."

"He's Johannes' son," Eleanor explained. "Knows the disappearing trick."

"And why did you pull me in, exactly?" I asked, though the mention of Venice had given me an inkling.

She made a complicated hand movement, and the dots vanished and resolved into a hazy image, moving through a crowd of people; it must be some kind of feed of what Markus was seeing, or had seen. For the first time, I began to appreciate the complexity of the magic that Eleanor dealt in.

"Do you recognize anyone?" she asked. "That man in the suit? I'll try to make it a little clearer."

She cleaned up the image a little. The man certainly did stand out, but only for his attire: a finely-tailored black suit that made him look more like a performer than a local or tourist. His features were otherwise unremarkable, but people were reacting to him with the interest that would normally accompany someone very handsome, or a minor celebrity that one is unable to place.

I looked at her and shook my head. "If you're thinking of the man on the dance floor, I don't know. I only saw him with a hood and a full mask on. But what makes you think it's him?"

"Just… a hunch, mostly. Ari noticed that his movement pattern seems as if he's looking for someone specific, so I was trying to think who a strange magician might be looking for. And from what Markus has seen so far, he's following women. The first thing that came to mind was that bastard from Venice."

No one says no to me. If it was him, I suspected it wasn't so much me he was interested in, as the fact that I'd been able to push back against his mental control. But the idea that he might have tracked me all the way to Germany because of it was unsettling to say the least. "The only way to know is to perform, and see if he tries anything."

Eleanor and Ari both nodded. "I agree. But we'll make sure you're well covered," she said.

It might not make much of a difference, if the man could dominate the will of anyone he liked. Although presumably – hopefully – he could only work on one person at a time. I looked at my watch: nearly nine-thirty, and we had planned to start around ten. "I'd better go and get ready. Could somebody walk me over there, just in case?"

Eleanor left the monitoring in Ari's hands and came out with me. "Don't worry too much," she said. "It's not like anybody can do much to you with eighty or ninety of us on site. Just want to keep an eye on things in case anyone leaves with him, visitors included."

"I can't believe the setup you have there." I needed to keep my mind off the man from Venice as much as possible if I was going to be able to pull it together and focus on my performance. "A lot of regular security outfits would kill for your talents."

She shrugged. "Magic's a tool, like any other. Some people use it in artistic ways; my brain works differently. Oh, hang on." Stopping by an alleyway between two rows of tents, she peered into the darkness. "Is that you?" Out of nowhere, a young man materialized; his face was unfamiliar, and I wondered how much of his time he spent invisible. "Markus, Heather's going to go on soon. Can you guys work out a signal or something, in case he tries anything?"

"You work with coloured lights. How controlled are you with the colour? Could you shoot a red light at him if need be?" Markus asked.

I thought about it. "If it is the same guy, and he's trying to push into my head, I'll need most of my energy to keep him out. Honestly, it's more likely that I wouldn't be able to keep the lights going at all."

Markus pursed his lips for a moment. "It's as good a sign as any. You won't see me, but if he's in your tent, I'll be within arm's reach of him." With that, he turned down the alley, vanishing like a mirage as he did so.

At the entry of the grey tent, Eleanor paused. "Are you going to tell Eric what's going on? He may not want to go ahead with the act."

"Tell me what?"

He did have an incredible knack for turning up out of nowhere; if I didn't know better, I would have thought he could do the vanishing trick as well. "I'll explain inside."

Eleanor had been mistaken. After hearing my brief explanation, Eric was all for going ahead – but it was also quite clear that if it was indeed the man from the Masquerade, he would have more to fear than just Eleanor's security detail. "After we're done – even if nothing happens – do not go anywhere without me," he concluded. "I'm serious. Not until we know what's going on."

It wasn't until I agreed to his condition that he was willing to light the exterior of the tent, dim the interior, and surround the two of us with the cloud of mist that preceded our routine. Then all there was to do was wait in silence and listen to the feet shuffling in around us. It was a strange feeling, quite different from being able to hide in the back of the tent as I'd done at Wéris, but this time it was comforting in a way – the closest I could come to actually vanishing into the ether.

As the performance began, the fog around us cleared just a little, as Eric drew some of it together into landscapes and creatures for me to illuminate. I could see that it was our biggest audience yet – the benches at capacity, the space behind ringed with standing figures – but it was impossible to make out faces. This was a good thing: less chance of getting distracted by looking for a particular individual in the crowd. The evening might go off without a hitch after all. But we had a new finale, which involved working the last of the mist into a swirl of multi-coloured stars: around us at first, then soaring up to the peak of the tent before raining down over the assembled audience. The catch with this was that it rendered us visible.

You.

It was so clear in my mind that it took me a moment to realize that no one had spoken. I didn't bother looking around; instead I drew inwards, trying to block the intrusion and send a message of my own. *Get out. Do not come back.* I was fairly sure my subconscious threw a significant profanity in for good measure. I had thought I would feel fear. I was wrong: it was anger. Unable to hold the mental block and keep up any other magic at the same time, I let the stars fade to grey.

And then all hell broke loose.

The audience's first clue that something was amiss came when a yell sounded, off to my right: invisible Markus must have indeed been within arm's reach. Perhaps more alarming for the unsuspecting onlookers was the sight of Eric barging through two rows of seated audience, the forgotten grey stars temporarily following him in a cloud that obscured my view of events. Standing there alone in the centre of the ring as shouting erupted at the back, I did the first thing that came to mind: I bowed. There was a smattering of applause, but most people were already hastening towards the exit, sensibly wanting to get away from the disturbance. There was a muffled curse, and the tent went completely black for a moment, which shifted the mood toward mild panic as people began to push and grope their way out before I managed to cast a low ambient light around the perimeter.

A smaller knot of people was pressing in around the commotion, trying to see what was happening. Some of these were magicians, but a few were visitors, young men who looked as though this were just another interesting late-night show. I tugged on the nearest familiar sleeve, which happened to be Gavin's. "Get them out of there, will you?"

As he began to herd the spectators out into the night, I tried to find my way through to see what was going on. Pushing past Luke and some of his friends and elbowing my way around someone else, I finally spied the man I had seen on Eleanor and Ari's display a little earlier. He was looking significantly the worse for wear, knocked on the ground with one sleeve of his suit torn at the shoulder and his mouth bleeding from a split lip. And yet, curiously, everything had gone quiet. Markus was visible, and Eric was backing away, his face strangely blank. It took me a second to realize what was going on.

"He's in your heads; pay attention," I snapped, then turned my full attention on the man, who was beginning to get to his feet. "You sit the hell down." I tried to push the command forward with my mind as well as my voice, but it was not to be quite that simple. He stood to his full height and narrowed his eyes at me.

"I suppose there's no convincing you to talk with me privately," he said. I could feel him around the edges of my mind, looking for a way in, but I managed to keep him at bay.

I must have drawn his full attention, though, because before I could respond, Eric punched him in the gut, causing him to double over and giving me a moment's mental reprieve. "She told you to sit down."

"Two of you, hold him," I instructed.

"You want to hit him?" somebody asked.

Truth be told, it was tempting. But I shook my head. "Just keep more than one person on him. He's trying to pull Jedi mind tricks on you; if you're ready, it's harder to do." I didn't know if that was actually true for everyone, but it seemed the right advice to give. "He's like Sébastien."

Dropping my ancestor's name got a few people's attention – including the man in the torn suit. "You know that name," I said, careful to keep my distance. "How?"

"I saw my father shoot him."

Whatever answer I might have expected, that wasn't it. Focused as I was on keeping the stranger from influencing my mind, it took me several seconds to process his words. Sébastien had been murdered sometime in the nineteen-thirties: shot by a jealous husband after having seduced one too many women. If this man was telling the truth, he had to be around eighty years old, though he didn't look much older than me. And it had to mean... "Your father didn't shoot Sébastien. Sébastien was your father." *Where did you think you got it?* I added the last on silently, amid murmurs from the crowd.

"I did not 'get' this from anyone!" he shrieked, making an attempt to break free of the hold that Markus and Eric had on his upper arms. "It is my gift, and mine alone! Until you. Stupid, common girl."

His emotional state seemed to be disorganizing his mental focus; I could think more clearly now. "You're a lunatic. And nobody calls me stupid."

Suddenly, I felt a sharp pain, like a knife to the centre of my forehead. I gasped and stepped back, putting my hand up to cover the spot, but it only lasted a moment; almost as soon as I flinched, Eric caught the man with an uppercut to the chin and he slumped forward, unconscious.

"Get him out of here," Eric said, handing off his responsibility for the dead weight to Ari and Gavin; along with Markus, they started dragging the man away by the arms, none too carefully. With the obvious drama over, some people left, while a few others clustered around to see if I was alright. I gave assurances that I was fine, just fine, until the tent was empty but for Eric and myself.

Only then did it all start to catch up with me. "He was pretty wrapped up in the idea that no one else can do what he does," I said, slumping down on a bench. "What was he planning to do, kill me?"

"Don't say that," Eric replied immediately. "Nobody would have let that happen."

"Sébastien was shot." The more I thought about it, the more real it became in my mind.

"Sébastien deserved it, to be quite frank. You don't. There's a big difference." He came and sat beside me, putting a steadying hand on my back. "And among their other talents, Eleanor and Ari are able to screen for weapons, which nobody could do back then. This guy didn't have any, apart from magic. I promised you once that you're basically safe here, and even though I never expected anything like tonight, I meant it. Now, come on; let's get out of here. We can find out tomorrow what they're going to do with the guy."

We made our way out of the tent, out of the grounds and up the hill towards Annika's house. Most of the trek was silent, until Eric paused at the garden gate. "I need to ask you something."

"What?"

"How long have you been able to read minds?"

I shook my head. "I can't read minds. I don't think that guy can, either, not really. I didn't know I could do anything like that at all until he started twisting my thoughts at the Masquerade. I just... I realized he was like Sébastien, and I thought that maybe I might have inherited enough of the skill to counteract it. Once or twice I could hear him saying something, inside my head, and I think I managed to do the same, but it's like... sending a message, not reading a book."

Eric nodded. "So you can't see what I'm thinking right now?"

For the sake of argument, I tried, exhausted though I was. "No. Not even a little."

"Good."

CHAPTER TWENTY

By noon the next day, the house was a hive of activity. Magicians were coming and going to find out more about the dust-up and to make sure that I was okay, Eric insisted on presiding over every step I took out of doors, and a scandalized Annika kept buzzing around, making continual pots of coffee and reiterating her shock that something untoward had happened to us in her hometown.

Despite the fact that news of the incident seemed to have spread far and wide, there was no further word about the perpetrator. "Claire just texted me: Ben's in a meeting with the elders," Eric told me, in a moment between visitors. "He'll know what's going on."

A little after two, Ben arrived at the door. After bidding Luke to clear off, and excusing himself more politely to Annika, he sat down at the table with me, Eric and Eleanor. "Our friend was shown the error of his ways last night," he said. "And we managed to learn a little about him. His name is Frederick Desrochers, and it seems you're probably right about him being Sébastien's son, though he doesn't look it. From what we got out of him, he was likely only two or three years old when his mother's husband shot

Sébastien down in front of him. Apparently he shot the mother afterwards as well."

I shuddered. "Small wonder if he grew up crazy."

"Spare us his tale of woe," Eric countered. "Where is he now, and what are we doing about him?"

Eleanor nodded. "Exactly."

"Yes, well, I'll come to the point." Ben looked around the table at each of us in turn. "First off, as you've probably guessed, we're moving on straight away. We'll pack up this afternoon and all go lay low at home for a week or so before we go travelling again. The moment we get back to Fernwood, Heather starts training with Mum and Dad."

We all looked at him blankly at that. "My parents used to do something like Eleanor's job, back in their day," Ben continued. "And though we've no relation to Sébastien, Mum has a trick or two of her own up her sleeve. They'll give Heather a few more tools to work with, should she ever run across trouble like that again."

I leaned forward, tired of being discussed in the third person. "And what about this Frederick?"

"Well." Ben drew the word out. "I believe he's been treated to a bit of a sleeping draught, and Ari and Markus are taking him for a ride in one of the vans. Depending how long he stays asleep, I think Ari said something about the Romanian countryside being lovely at this time of year." He chuckled to himself. "And Sofia's done something to him. She wouldn't say what – she never does say much – but I suspect he'll be less keen to track us down in future."

Eric's mouth was still set in a line. "So he's not gone entirely."

Ben held his hands out. "What would you have us do? Kill him in cold blood? It's not a perfect solution, but it's the best we've got. Get him out of the way, give him a disincentive to return, and make sure Heather has a few more options in case he ever shows his face again. But for the record, darling, you handled yourself exceptionally," he added, patting my hand. "So did you, Eleanor. That tracking system of yours is a wonder."

"And me?" Eric asked, frowning.

"You did exactly what I would've done," Ben replied, with a grin. "And I can't give much higher praise than that."

By the time we all walked down together, the tents had already been packed up, the last few odds and ends just being loaded into the two remaining vans. "I suppose Claire will need to go along with you, Eleanor, and collect her car. The rest will come on at their leisure," Ben said. "I'll give you the details where we're to meet next."

I watched over his shoulder as he wrote out the magician's card for her: *Uig, Skye, November 24.*

"Back to Scotland?" I asked. "I like the sound of that."

Eleanor shook her head, tucking the card in her bag. "You know it'll be dark at three-thirty and probably blowing a gale every day, right?"

I looked around at the space under the trees, now bearing no hint of how it had looked the night before. "After the last twenty-four hours, I think a bit of weather is the least of my concerns. And I'm ready for a change of scenery."

"If you say so." Setting her bags down, she raised her eyebrows at me. "Are you coming in the van as well?"

"No. Not yet." When they all turned to look at me, I continued, the idea only really taking shape as the words came out of my mouth. "It's a full moon again in a couple of days and the

Black Forest is practically around the corner. I want to do the Magician's Walk again."

Eric looked at me as if I had taken leave of my senses. "With that guy still running around, you want to go out in the forest in the middle of the night by yourself?"

His point was valid, but the more I thought about it, the more I knew I needed to do it. "He's as far away as he's liable to get, and if he is still looking for me he's going to be looking for the troupe, not combing a hundred miles of random forest like he's a search-and-rescue team. Ben, you told me people sometimes do the Walk again if they feel like they need it. I know it's only been a month, but with everything that's gone on in the past few weeks, I need to do this. Do you know how to help me?"

Ben held my gaze for several seconds, then nodded. "Fine. But let's do this tomorrow night and have it over with."

CHAPTER TWENTY-ONE

"Well, you know what to do, darling." The sun was going down and we were standing in a clearing in the Black Forest. Three of us, since Eric seemed determined to continue acting as my bodyguard until I headed back to Ireland. Ben put a hand on my shoulder. "Are you ready?"

"As ready as I'm liable to get."

Eric gave me a resigned sort of grin. "Good luck."

Ben shook his head. "She doesn't need luck."

Turning his back, he circled the clearing, speaking in a low voice, just as Daniel had the last time. And just like the last time, a faint sheen appeared on the ground in a gap between the trees, marking my way onwards.

Having done the Magician's Walk just weeks before, I wasn't surprised this time by the monotonous, seemingly endless march through the dark woods. I still wasn't entirely sure what had prompted me to try it again, and some back corner of my mind imagined finding Don Ross, Granny Chrissie, and John Heyward once more and having them question why I was back so soon. But when I finally saw movement ahead, it was something quite different.

The people I had met the last time had been solid, substantial; what I saw now was hazy, a translucent scene like a movie flickering against the forest backdrop. Ironically, the solid figures had all been deceased, and I could say for certain that I was now looking at the living, because what I saw was myself. I watched my own figure bend down and drop to a seated position somewhere near the forest floor, and only then did I realize that there was a second person in the scene: Sofia, the elder known as the oracle. Why would the walk show me this?

I spent a few moments trying to analyze the scene, before I decided that it made more sense to simply observe. It was a recreation – not an exact replaying – of the first moment I had stepped into the oracle's tent at Callanish. "You will learn something about yourself," she said, just as I remembered. "And have to make a choice." With that, the illusion began to fade. Clearly, this was the message I had been intended to receive, but why?

Before I could think too much about it, I heard a voice. "You have learned something else about yourself."

I looked around the clearing, but saw no one. The speaker was male; not Desrochers, thankfully, but also not a voice I recognized at all. "Who are you?"

Laughter was the response. "You have learned something," the voice repeated, still apparently disembodied. "Something new. A legacy, that you may yet turn to your own advantage." There was an accent that I could not quite place, and he sounded amused. Something told me it was at my expense. "And you will have to make a choice."

"What choice? Who are you?" For the first time, I began to wonder if I had made a mistake in coming.

"If you do not have it already, you will know the answer soon enough. To both questions."

And then there was silence, broken after a few minutes by the call of a bird heralding the coming dawn. My long walk to this place must have carried me in a circle, for when I listened more carefully I found I could hear a low conversation not too far away: the welcome sound of familiar voices, Eric and Ben. But just as I was turning to walk back in that direction, I heard the stranger once more. But this time, his voice came from inside my own head.

Which way will you choose?

I stepped out of the forest and into the first rays of the morning sun, the question unanswered.

ABOUT THE AUTHOR

Lori Zuppinger is a historian by day and writer by night. She lives in Toronto with her husband, son, and cat. (Yes, the cat is still a polydactyl and still grouchy. Thank you for asking.) When she has a free moment, she is usually heading out to a concert, playing board games, or wondering why the owl with her Hogwarts letter is so very delayed.

Lori can be found at:
@ratherawkward (Twitter)
@escapistwriter (Instagram)
@lorizuppinger.author (Facebook)

Books in the Magicians' Card series:

The Magicians' Card
The Magician's Walk
The Magician's Shadow (coming soon)

www.ingramcontent.com/pod-product-compliance
Lightning Source LLC
Chambersburg PA
CBHW020644180626
46816CB00003B/1118